Please renew or return items by the date shown on your receipt

www.hertfordshire.gov.uk/libraries

Renewals and enquiries: 0300 123 **4049**

Textphone for hearing or   0300 123 **4041**
speech impaired users:

L32 11.16

A LORD IN DISGUISE

When Lord Edward Stonham kills his opponent in a duel, he is forced to flee and take on a false identity. As country gentleman Edward Trevelyan, he recruits Penelope Bradshaw, the eldest daughter of a well-born widow fallen on hard times, to be his housekeeper. While they are initially secretive about their personal circumstances, they soon become confidantes. But Edward is not in a position to offer for Penny's hand in marriage, so they can never declare their love. Are they prepared to ignore propriety in order to be together?

Books by Fenella J. Miller
in the Linford Romance Library:

THE RETURN OF LORD RIVENHALL
A COUNTRY MOUSE
A RELUCTANT BRIDE
A DANGEROUS DECEPTION
MISTAKEN IDENTITY
LORD ATHERTON'S WARD
LADY CHARLOTTE'S SECRET
CHRISTMAS AT HARTFORD HALL
MISS SHAW & THE DOCTOR
TO LOVE AGAIN
MISS BANNERMAN AND THE DUKE
MISS PETERSON & THE COLONEL
WED FOR A WAGER
AN UNEXPECTED ENCOUNTER
HOUSE OF DREAMS
THE DUKE'S PROPOSAL
THE DUKE'S RELUCTANT BRIDE
THE DUKE & THE VICAR'S
DAUGHTER
LORD ILCHESTER'S INHERITANCE
LADY EMMA'S REVENGE
CHRISTMAS AT CASTLE ELRICK
A MOST UNUSUAL CHRISTMAS
THE RECLUSIVE DUKE

FENELLA J. MILLER

A LORD IN DISGUISE

Complete and Unabridged

LINFORD
Leicester

First published in Great Britain in 2019

First Linford Edition
published 2019

A catalogue record for this book is available
from the British Library.

ISBN 978–1–4448–4066–7

Published by
F. A. Thorpe (Publishing)
Anstey, Leicestershire

Set by Words & Graphics Ltd.
Anstey, Leicestershire
Printed and bound in Great Britain by
T. J. International Ltd., Padstow, Cornwall

This book is printed on acid-free paper

1

The clearing in the forest was deserted, apart from the two horses who stood patiently waiting for the duel to be over. The early-morning mist swirled around their feet. Edward knew this was a catastrophic error on his part. He had tried to call it off but his opponent, Lord Jasper Bentley, had refused. His second, Lord Richard Dunwoody, shifted uneasily beside him.

'Let's forget it, Edward; better to be called a coward than arrested for duelling.'

'I should not have let myself be provoked by him. The feud between our families has gone on long enough. I should have walked away.'

'I was there — he insulted your betrothed. He all but called her a light-skirt. He left you no choice.'

Edward stiffened. There was a definite

sound of a carriage approaching. Too late to back out now. 'I'm not going to do more than wing him. I doubt he'll hit me; he's notorious for being a poor shot.'

'Can't think why he chose pistols. He would have done better with a rapier.'

The carriage was just visible through the mist. He saw one coachman on the box, and three men descended. Good God — Bentley had brought a saw-bones with him.

'I sincerely hope that neither of us will need his services. You had better go and check the weapons he has brought.'

His friend strode over, and the murmur of voices carried across the empty space. If the mist didn't lift, it would be foolhardy to continue, as they would be unable to see each other clearly. Then the sun rose above the treetops and the place was bathed in magical golden light. Hardly appropriate for what was about to take place.

Lady Jemima Babbage, his beloved future wife, knew nothing about this, and he hoped she never would. He was the luckiest man in Christendom to have her for his bride. They had been engaged for three months and their nuptials were to take place at the end of June, in two months' time.

Richard walked back with a pistol in his hand. 'Shall we get this over with? We need to be away from here before the constables become aware of what is taking place.'

Edward shrugged off his jacket and handed it over. He took the weapon and checked it was loaded. He was an excellent shot, and was confident his bullet would do no more than graze the shoulder of his opponent. The matter would be settled, and they could both ride away relatively unscathed.

Papa was aware, and he had his full support. The feud between the Bentleys and the Stonhams had begun fifty years ago when Edward's grandfather had eloped with the intended bride of Bentley's grandfather. The fact that the grandsons of the two perpetrators were about to face each other because of something that happened so long ago was ludicrous. What had happened was nothing to do with either of them — high time the disagreement was put aside.

The two seconds paced out the required distance, and he took his place. He stood sideways, making himself the smallest target possible. Bentley did the same. There was the usual count of three, and he flinched as the other man fired. The bullet missed.

Edward steadied his breathing. Held his arm still and pulled the trigger. To his horror, Bentley staggered back clutching his chest, and his white shirt was suddenly a hideous red. His instinct was to run forward and offer his assistance, but Richard grabbed his elbow.

'Away — we must go. If he dies, you're for the gallows. I can hear someone galloping towards us. The authorities must have discovered us.'

He pulled on his topcoat and raced

for his horse. He should have thrown the pistol away, but still had it in his hand as he vaulted into the saddle. He shoved the weapon into his pocket, his boots into the stirrup irons, and kicked his stallion into a gallop.

They travelled across country, jumping the hedges and ditches, and arrived in a skid of gravel outside his family home an hour later. He tossed the reins to Richard and hurtled into the house.

There was not a minute to lose. He would have to flee the country and risk being captured by Napoleon's troops if he went to France, or take a boat to the colonies. The authorities would be informed and, despite the fact that his father was the Earl of Rushmere, and he his sole heir, he would be arrested.

Better to be in exile the rest of his life than bring such ignominy on his family name. The woman he loved was now lost to him, and all because of his own stupidity.

He was about to ascend the stairs when his father called him back. 'My study, son; we can talk there.'

When Edward explained what had transpired, his father was as shocked as he. 'I can only surmise that the weapon you were given was not of true aim. Too late to repine. We must make the best of things as they are.'

'At least if I am overseas, I cannot be hanged if the wretched man dies. Forgive me, Father, but I must not delay if I am to be away before I am taken.'

'I have another suggestion for you, my boy. When you told me about this duel, I prepared for this eventuality. Your dear departed mother inherited a substantial estate in Suffolk, a county somewhere in East Anglia, and it has been occupied by a tenant for years. Recently the old man died and the property is vacant. You will assume a new persona and take over this place. Although we will never be able to meet again in this lifetime — it would be far too risky to do so — at least I shall know you are alive and well.'

'I don't know what to say. I am still

reeling from the shock of what happened. Quickly, can you tell me everything I need to know about this place?'

'First I must tell you your new name. In future you will be known as Edward Trevelyan, Esquire. You had not expected to inherit this property, had no monetary expectations, and are thrilled to find yourself a wealthy landowner.' He pointed to a stack of documents on the desk. 'Take these and read them on your journey. They will tell you everything.'

Edward poured himself a large glass of brandy. His father was, as always, three steps ahead of the game. 'I cannot take my valet — he might be recognised — and neither can I take any of my horses or hounds. Therefore, I shall arrive with meagre belongings and start afresh.' He drained his drink and closed the gap between them. 'I shall miss you, Papa. I hope you can forgive me for ruining our lives.'

His parent embraced him — not something he did often — and cleared his throat noisily. 'I have set up a bank account for you in the local market town, Ipswich. You must travel by stage and take only the barest minimum with you. Godspeed, my boy. I hope that one day you might meet and marry a young lady and provide us with an heir. You cannot inherit, but my grandson will be able to do so.'

The thought of becoming involved with another young lady filled him with horror. He had never thought to fall in love, had thought this a flummery business, but then he had met Jemima and everything was suddenly different. He swallowed a lump in his throat. 'Can I ask you to contact my betrothed and explain the situation?'

'Of course, of course. Now, do not delay any longer. I have arranged for one of the grooms who is about your height and build to travel to Dover in our carriage, accompanied by your valet. They will take the next ship that sails, and hopefully this will be enough to put the constables on the wrong track.'

'I shall slip out through the trades-men's route. It is no more than a mile or two along the track to the toll road. I'll take the next coach that comes.'

His father had thought of everything. Sending a decoy to France was a masterstroke. Bates, his manservant, was clever, and the two of them would dispense with the disguise at the earliest possible opportunity before making their way back as common folk.

As he was changing from his elegant ensemble, the pistol bumped against his thigh. It might come in useful, so he pulled it out of his pocket and dropped it into the bottom of the battered carpetbag that had been put by for him to use. Bates had laid out a set of garments that normally would only be worn *in extremis*. They would be ideal in the circumstances.

The sound of the carriage outside on the turning circle made him move to the window. He smiled ruefully as the groom who was to play the part of himself strode from the house. He was wearing his beaver pulled low over his eyes and had the collar of his greatcoat turned up. Bates hurried along behind, carrying two large bags. They jumped into the carriage, the door slammed, and it thundered off down the drive.

The family crest was emblazoned in gold on the side of this vehicle, and at the speed it was travelling it could not fail to be noticed by anyone who saw it.

Bates had already put in his shaving gear, a bag of golden guineas, two shirts that had seen better days, a spare pair of breeches and two pairs of stockings. This would be sufficient until he had established himself as the new owner of this estate and was able to purchase fresh garments.

He looked down at his boots and decided that these he would keep; even a young gentleman with few expectations might have a decent pair of Hessians.

★   ★   ★

'Penelope Bradshaw, I absolutely forbid you to do so.'

'Mama, I cannot see a viable alternative to my applying for the position as housekeeper at Ravenswood Hall.' Penny smiled patiently. Her mother was still living in the past, in the heady days when they had owned and resided at Bradshaw Manor and lived in the lap of luxury. All that had changed when her younger brother Benedict had been lost at sea along with dear Papa a year and a half ago. The estate had been entailed and an obnoxious distant cousin had inherited everything. They now lived in straitened circumstances on a small annuity in the village of Nettlested.

'You are a Bradshaw; you do not come from the servant classes. Your poor father would be turning in his grave to hear you say you intend to apply to be a housekeeper.'

'Mama, we can barely manage on the pittance we have. I have two younger sisters who will never find themselves

11

suitable husbands if I don't do something to improve matters. It is too late to complain: I delivered my application yesterday.'

Her mother sniffed noisily and dabbed her eyes with her lace handkerchief. 'I shall never recover from the shame.' She pursed her lips and added, 'Exactly how much will you be recompensed for giving up your time in this menial manner?'

'I intend to ask for twelve guineas a year, plus being allowed to supplement my income with food from the kitchen garden and larder.'

'That is almost satisfactory, Penelope. I don't suppose you will be able to ask for anything in advance?'

'It shall be one of my stipulations, Mama; do not worry on that account. Charlotte, being the daughter of the rector, has been able to supply me with all the information I need. The new owner of the estate, one Edward Trevelyan, did not expect to inherit, and has no knowledge of how such a substantial establishment should be run. The old gentleman who has been living there for the past thirty years had only the barest minimum of staff, and the place is sadly run-down. I shall be able to restore it to its former glory. After all, did I not run Bradshaw Manor successfully for you?'

'You did indeed, my love. As you know, I have always been in indifferent health and unable to fulfil my responsibilities. Your dear papa understood how fragile I am and never asked me to overtax myself.'

Penny hid her smile behind her hand. Her mother was as robust as any woman of her age might be, but was also indolent and not inclined to take responsibility for anything. It had fallen on her own shoulders to run the house whilst her father and brother travelled on business to India and other exotic places. It had also been Penny who had replaced the governess in educating her younger sisters after the staff had been released and the family had moved to this dilapidated house.

From the racket coming from the music room — a misnomer if ever there was one, as there were no musical instruments to be seen — she was failing dismally in that role. Her sisters were lively, intelligent young ladies and were running wild. This was why she had thought to apply for the position at Ravenswood. She was hoping that when Matilda, seventeen years of age, found herself in charge she would rise to the occasion and begin to behave with the decorum expected of a young lady.

After all, they were members of the aristocracy, even if they were at the bottom of the pile. Her father had been Sir Bernard Bradshaw, her mother was still Lady Bradshaw; their circumstances had changed, but they were still well-born. She hoped her pedigree would be an asset rather than a hindrance when it came to her application.

Mr Trevelyan had arrived a week ago. Her application had been delivered two days back. If he was interested in employing her, then she should hear today.

The weather was remarkably clement for the beginning of May, more like late summer than late spring. Despite the shabbiness of the house, the grounds were looking their best. They had brought with them four ancient retainers who were too old to continue in employment for the new owners of their ancestral home. Three of these were outside workers, and so they pruned and clipped and planted, thus making the gardens attractive and allowing Penny to fill the house with blooms. The fourth servant had been the butler, and he continued in that role although they did not really require his services anymore.

They had no livestock, if you did not count the dozen chickens in the yard at the back, or the two cats, and one very large scruffy mongrel that had been in residence when they arrived. She also employed a widow and her two daughters who had been in a similar position to them — evicted from their tied cottage when the man of the house had died.

Penny had taken to pulling back her hair in a most unbecoming way in an attempt to make herself look older. She was also wearing her plainest gown, a dull grey cotton in the old-fashioned style. She had a wardrobe full of pretty dresses with the high waist, but these would not do if she was to work for her living.

An unexpected hush from her sisters gave her pause. Then the two of them erupted into the drawing room. 'Penny, there's a gentleman strolling up our drive. I think he must be Mr Trevelyan come to see you about the job.'

'Then I shall receive him in the library. Kindly keep your mother company until he has gone.' They both knew that what she really meant was not to allow their parent to intrude on the interview.

There was barely time for her to

settle herself behind the desk when she heard a loud knock on the front door. It would take Foster an age to get there, and she hoped the visitor would not abandon hope and go away.

A full ten minutes later, the decrepit butler staggered into the doorway. 'A Mr Edward Trevelyan to see you, Miss Bradshaw.' The old man was wheezing horribly; Penny forgot she was supposed to be sitting behind a desk looking efficient, and ran to his aid.

Before she reached him, Mr Trevelyan was there, and put his arm around Foster's shoulders. 'Allow me, sir, to assist you to a chair.'

'Thank you; I shall fetch him a brandy. We keep some for medicinal purposes in the bureau.'

The drink seemed to help, and the horrible rasping noise stopped. Foster's colour began to return to his ashen cheeks. 'I'm perfectly well now, thank you, Miss Bradshaw. I apologise for my — '

'You'll do no such thing, Foster. I

told you to stay in bed today and take care of yourself. We shall get you there now, and Tilly shall look after you until you are well again.'

The gentleman she had hoped to work for nodded. 'Come along, Mr Foster. Put your arm around my neck and I'll get you to your bedchamber.'

As they emerged from the library, Matilda was waiting, looking anxious. 'I don't think dear Foster should be upstairs in the attic. I've had Tilly prepare the bedchamber in the apartment downstairs. He'll be far more comfortable there.'

'Thank you, Mattie. I should have thought of that myself. Mr Trevelyan, if you would be so kind as to follow me, it is just at the end of this passageway.'

She left her sister to settle the patient and then led their visitor back to the library. 'I do apologise for inconveniencing you, sir, but the welfare of my staff must always come first.'

He smiled, and for the first time she was aware that he was an attractive gentleman. Fair hair and blue eyes did not usually appeal to her, but the facts that he was also more than two yards high and had a satisfactory breadth of shoulder made him very personable.

'There is absolutely no need to apologise, Miss Bradshaw. Might I be seated?'

She flushed painfully at this omission. 'Yes, please do.'

He waited politely until she too had found herself a seat. 'I am assuming that you are living in straitened circumstances because of a family catastrophe?'

It had not been her intention to reveal too much about herself, but she could hardly refuse after he had been so helpful. She explained, concluding with: 'Therefore, you will see that I am an ideal candidate for the position of housekeeper. At the moment you have no staff; I know everyone in the vicinity and can appoint your household for you.'

'I had come here with the intention of offering you the position, but now I have met you I think it would be unwise. You are an eligible young lady, so becoming a servant is not acceptable.'

She jumped to her feet in agitation. 'What is not acceptable, sir, is being unable to put food on the table for my family and dependents. I am unmarriageable, but my sisters are not. I'm hoping that once you are entertaining, I might find them suitable partners amongst your guests.'

His eyebrows rose, and she wished the words unspoken.

2

Unmarriageable? Edward was about to correct her on that erroneous assumption, but decided it would be unwise in the circumstances. Miss Bradshaw might construe his comments as having an interest in her himself, which was as far from the truth as it could be.

The girl was certainly pretty, though not at all in the common way. She was taller and thinner than was considered fashionable in the *ton*, and her hair was an ordinary mid-brown, but her eyes were quite extraordinary. Huge, lustrous and an amazing mix of green and brown.

Her family might be impecunious, but they were obviously genteel. She was staring at him, and he realised he hadn't responded to her last remark.

'I agree, Miss Bradshaw, that your sisters must be introduced to local society. I have no inkling how to set about this arduous task. I am not accustomed to moving in the highest circles; I was a clerk in a London office when I heard about my inheritance.'

She resumed her seat and waited politely for him to continue. He hated to lie to her, but had no choice. His old life was gone; there was nothing he could do to restore his fortune . . . but he could help this family. Doing so would give him a practical purpose and prevent him from dwelling on what was lost. 'Therefore, I suggest that you and your family move in with me as soon as the house is habitable. If Mrs Brad-shaw — '

'I beg your pardon, sir, but it is Lady Bradshaw. My father was Sir Bernard Bradshaw, of Bradshaw Manor.'

She said this as if he was supposed to know of whom she spoke. He tried to look intelligent, but from her expression had failed dismally.

'It is I who must apologise for miscalling her. Lady Bradshaw will be

sufficient chaperone to make it acceptable for the three of you to be there.
Then you can take over running the
house, and act as my hostess, but you
will not be labelled as the housekeeper.'

'That is a most generous offer, Mr
Trevelyan. I think you had better meet
the other members of my family before
you make a firm decision. I fear you will
be getting the worst of the bargain.'

She smiled, and turned from ordinary to quite beautiful. He was shocked
that he could react in this way so soon
after losing the woman he loved. He
was a red-blooded male, and as such
could hardly be castigated for noticing
a desirable woman.

He pushed such unsuitable thoughts
from his head. He must find himself a
mistress as soon as might be. He had
given up the ladybird he had kept in
luxury in London on his betrothal to
Jemima. He had remained celibate
since then, and this must be the reason
he was having lustful thoughts about
this young lady.

'If you would care to come with me, I will introduce you formally to Mattie — Matilda — who is seventeen years of age; and Elizabeth — known as Beth — who is a year her junior. They are both wild and behave most indecorously, but are the dearest girls, kind and intelligent and funny. My mama considers herself to be ailing, but is as hearty as I am. She has, however, a sweet nature, and never a cross word to say about anyone or anything.'

He was amused by her summation of her family and was eager to make their acquaintance. The older of the two sisters, Matilda, he had briefly glimpsed, and from what he had noticed she was shorter and rounder than Miss Bradshaw. She also had abundant blonde curls — again quite different from her older sister.

As they entered the drawing room, Lady Bradshaw raised a languid hand from her position on the chaise longue. He saw at once where the younger girls got their looks, as they were the image of their parent. She was an attractive woman for her age, with not a grey hair in sight. The younger girl curtsied politely and he nodded in return.

He cursed inwardly. He was supposed to be unfamiliar with the behaviour of society and should have offered to shake hands. Too late to repine.

'I'm delighted to make your acquaintance, my lady, and hope I will find you in better health very soon.'

'I thank you, Mr Trevelyan, but I am a martyr to several ailments and rarely able to get about.'

Miss Bradshaw was unimpressed by this statement. 'Mama, Mr Trevelyan has suggested that we all move into Ravenswood when he has finished the reparations. He is unfamiliar with the ways of our world and is hoping to learn how to go on from us.'

Her ladyship swung her legs to the floor, looking remarkably well for someone who had been ailing a moment before.

Miss Bradshaw continued, 'Obviously, we cannot do so if you are not well enough to take your part. I am to organise the household, and he will expect you to act as his hostess and be chaperone to my sisters, otherwise we cannot go.'

This was a masterly stroke and had the desired effect.

'How long will it take to complete the repairs, Mr Trevelyan?'

'A month; possibly a little longer, my lady.'

'In which case, sir, I can guarantee I will be fully recovered by then. Your suggestion is acceptable to me and you will not regret it.'

There was nothing else to say. He bowed several times and heard the younger girl snigger. Satisfied he had made himself appear an idiot, and in need of instruction in the ways of the world, he backed out as if leaving royalty.

The sound of girlish laughter followed him, and he was smiling to himself when he reached the front door, which had been left open.

'That was doing it too brown, sir. You are as familiar with how to behave as I am.'

All desire to laugh left him, and he turned to face Penny, who was far too observant.

'No, do not poker up at me. I shall not ask why you are pretending to be someone you are not. As far as I'm concerned, you are a godsend, and I will not do anything to jeopardise our good fortune. I give you my word that I'll not reveal your secret to anyone.'

He could do one of two things: act the buffoon, or admit she was right. He decided on the latter — it would be a relief to be himself with one person at least.

'Thank you, Miss Bradshaw, for your discretion. I cannot tell you why I am living here or reveal my true name; but suffice it to say, to do so might well prove fatal.'

Her eyes widened and he wished the

words unspoken. She was a country girl, gently born but not versed in London society. She recovered immediately and looked over her shoulder to ensure they were private.

'A duel in which your opponent died, perhaps?'

He did not agree or disagree. How could she possibly have worked it out so quickly? 'We cannot discuss this here. Could I prevail upon you to visit me tomorrow under the pretence of selecting fabric and such nonsense for the house?'

'I will come alone at ten o'clock.' She flashed another of her amazing smiles. 'I fear you will be obliged to allow me to actually interfere with your refurbishment. I have excellent taste, unlike my mama, who is a slavish follower of whatever is fashionable in the *ton*. I promise I shall not insist on either a Chinese or Egyptian theme.'

'I'm relieved to hear you say so, Miss Bradshaw, for I cannot abide furniture with the feet of an animal.'

They were now on the front step. 'Please will you address me by my given name? I am Penelope, Penny to my family and close acquaintances.'

'I should be delighted to. I am Edward, but Teddy to my family and close acquaintances.'

To his astonishment she giggled, a most unlikely sound from someone who looked so serious. 'I shall call you Edward, sir. I cannot possibly call you Teddy, as it does not suit you one jot.'

Her eyes were sparkling, and he believed he might come to like her very well when they were better acquainted. He walked back to his new abode with a spring in his step. Not only was he to have companions in his banishment, but he now had someone he could be himself with.

★　★　★

Penny closed the door and almost skipped back to the drawing room. She had promised not to reveal what she

29

knew to anyone, but she had not agreed not to try and discover who he was. Mr Trevelyan was a gentleman, born to lead; if he had been an articled clerk, then she was the Queen of Sheba.

They could not afford a daily paper, but her bosom beau Charlotte was allowed to read her father's newspaper when he had done with it. If someone important had been killed in the duel, then it would have been reported in the paper. Edward had been in residence a week or more, so the event must have taken place a while before then.

Mama was in high alt at the thought of moving from this draughty, damp and dismal house to somewhere almost as grand as Bradshaw Manor.

'To think that I almost forbade you to apply for the position of housekeeper. My darling girl, you are the saviour of this family. We shall be able to live in comfort once again, and it is all down to you.'

'I must speak to all of you seriously about this. We will be living with a stranger for the sole purpose of introducing him to local society and teaching him how to behave appropriately. At any time he could send us packing, so we must all be on our best behaviour and make ourselves indispensable.'

'I understand perfectly, my love. From this moment on, I shall make more effort to be useful. I give you my word I will not lie about all day eating sweetmeats once we are there.' Mama now looked directly at the girls. 'You two will curb your wild ways and behave as you should in future. You will mind what your sister says to you, and practise your watercolours and playing on the pianoforte.'

Mattie and Beth exchanged glances. 'We promise!' said the latter. 'We might be silly, but we are not stupid. An opportunity like this will never come along again, and we have no intention of wasting it. We will be the epitome of good behaviour from this moment on.'

Penny laughed. 'Do not promise something none of you can fulfil! All I ask is that you do your best and do not give Mr Trevelyan cause to send us away. I am going to see Charlotte and give her the good news.'

They didn't question this, as she often walked across the fields to visit the rectory when she had finished her daily tasks.

As she strolled through the fields listening to the birdsong, she considered in more detail how their lives were going to change. In future they would be dressed appropriately, and the pretty gowns in her closet could come out once more. She loved to ride — was it possible she would be able to take up this enjoyable pastime again?

Mrs Rushton was on her way out to do good works in the neighbourhood when she arrived. 'Charlotte is helping Mr Rushton with his correspondence, but I'm sure she will be happy to see you and escape from that onerous duty.'

'I have so much to tell her, but I won't keep her long.'

Her friend must have seen her

coming down the path, and was already on the stairs waiting for them both to retire to her bedchamber, where they could have some privacy.

'Charlotte, I cannot wait to tell you what has transpired. You will not believe it.'

Indeed, the news that they were to move to the grandest house in the neighbourhood quite silenced her normally talkative companion. When she had recovered her wits, however, she had plenty to say on the subject.

'How serendipitous, Penny, for you and your family. I believe you will be too grand to keep up our friendship once you are installed there.'

Although she had only known Charlotte since they had moved into the village, they had seen each other every day of the past eighteen months. 'That's fustian, and you know it. I shall be living a deal nearer to you, so it will be even easier to meet.'

For the next half hour, she was grilled about the appearance, demeanour and eligibility of Mr Trevelyan, and she thought she was able to answer the questions without arousing any suspicions. It would not have done to have asked for the newspapers directly; she must not do anything out of the ordinary. A ruse had occurred to her on her walk to the rectory, and she now put this into action.

'It is so long since I have mixed in the upper echelons of local society, indeed of any society, that I am sadly out of date with what is going on. He will expect me to be *au fait* with all the *on dits*, and I was wondering if your father would allow me to borrow his old newspapers.'

'Of course he will. I shall collect them from the study when you leave.'

Penny was already on her feet, her mission accomplished satisfactorily. 'I fear I must leave now; you have your father's correspondence to complete, and I have a deal of organising to put in hand before we can transfer to our new home. I am to go there tomorrow and advise him on furnishings, fabric and paint, and I am not knowledgeable on the subjects.'

'Then I have exactly what you need. Mama has just recently been sent half a dozen copies of *Ackermann's Repository*. They are fairly recent publications and will have everything you need to bring you up to date with current fashion.'

Charlotte also lent her a basket to put the journals and newspapers in. With this over her arm, Penny returned at a brisk pace, eager to begin her research. She returned home expecting the house to be busy, with her sisters and mother eagerly writing lists and thinking about the benefits of this new arrangement.

The house was silent and her heart sank to her boots. What disaster had befallen the family now, when things were finally improving?

She put the basket down and looked in the drawing room, music room and dining room, but all were empty. Gathering up her skirts, she ran upstairs, and immediately heard the murmur of voices coming from her mama's bedchamber.

On pushing open the door, she was shocked to find her parent in bed and actually looking extremely unwell. Her two sisters were hovering anxiously at the bedside. 'What is wrong?'

'Mama had a bilious attack, Penny. She is much better now,' Mattie said.

Their mother opened her eyes. 'I am sorry to alarm you, girls. It was the shock and excitement that caused my nausea. I used to have these attacks in my youth, but I thought myself immune to such unpleasantness now I am old.'

'You are in your prime, Mama. Two-and-forty is no great age. Mrs Rushton is older than you and has three young children in the nursery.'

This made them all smile. 'Good heavens! You should not mention such things, my love. I shall be well tomorrow but need to sleep now. Run along, girls, and let me rest.'

They had no personal attendants

nowadays when once they had had servants aplenty. Mama had been the youngest daughter of a wealthy lord and had lived a luxurious life until they had moved here. She had never complained about being obliged to look after herself, but it must have been hard for her to adjust.

Tomorrow she would discuss such matters with Edward and suggest he should employ a personal maid for Mama as well as a valet for himself. His neckcloth had been untidy, and his topcoat in need of a brush and a damp cloth. No doubt he was also unused to dressing himself.

There was no opportunity to peruse the journals and newspapers until the house was quiet that night. As a rule, they went to bed at dark to save candles; but as this was no longer essential, she could stay up and read them now.

She put the magazines to one side — she would look at them first thing in the morning before she set out. She was far more interested in discovering the identity of Mr Trevelyan. She selected the oldest copy and assiduously read through each page. There was no mention of a duel or of anybody dying from their injuries.

The third paper she opened had what she was looking for. There was an announcement of the untimely death of one Lord Jasper Bentley. The use of this word made her scour the rest of the paper, and she was rewarded by a brief article saying that Lord Edward Stonham had been seen to flee the country after killing Lord Bentley in a duel. Could this be him? Surely it should have been more difficult to discover his identity? If she had done so, then surely the authorities would be able to find him?

Then she considered the problem in more depth. There would hardly be a plethora of men involved in duels on any given day, so it had been easy for her. However, as the paper stated that Lord Edward had fled the country, presumably they would not be looking for him elsewhere. It would be far more difficult if you started at the other end of the conundrum.

Although he acted as if he was an easy-going sort of person, she rather thought he was the opposite. Would her curiosity make him retract his offer?

3

Edward was sleeping in the drawing room, as this was the only chamber with sound windows and no holes in the ceiling. When he had blindly said the house would be ready for habitation in a month, he had been grossly underestimating the amount of work that would be needed to restore it to its former magnificence.

He had half a dozen men repairing the roof, another half dozen working on the grounds . . . but if things were to be done in so short a space of time, he would need to employ several dozen, and he had no notion where to find them.

Miss Bradshaw — no, she would be *Penny* to him now — could possibly find him the labourers he needed. It was in her interest to get things done speedily. When he had visited the bank on his way here, he had been gratified to find he had sufficient funds to restore a dozen properties.

Tomorrow was time enough to worry about such things. Tonight, he would ride down to the local hostelry and see what was on offer. So far he had been living on short commons indeed, for there were only two servants employed and neither of them were particularly efficient.

The carriage and team he had purchased was adequate for his needs, but if he was to ride around his properties, he would need a decent nag. Somehow he rather thought that Penny would be able to help him with that as well.

For the first time today, he thought about his lost love. Jemima would not have the first notion about any of these matters, and he had always loved this about her; loved the fact that he would be her protector and guide her in everything she did. It had not occurred to him that there might be a young lady of similar status to himself who was so self-sufficient she appeared to have no need for any gentleman in her life.

One thing he had discovered was that the wine cellar was well-stocked, and he had drunk himself into a stupor with excellent claret most evenings. Tonight he had only a couple of glasses. He wanted to have his wits about him tomorrow morning if he was to somehow mislead that perspicacious young lady.

★　★　★

It had taken him several botched attempts before he could shave himself without endangering his life. Today he would make an effort with his appearance, tie his neckcloth in a waterfall, and give his breeches and topcoat some attention too. He must find himself a competent valet and set about replacing his wardrobe. There must be a tailor in Ipswich who could make him something respectable. He had no intention of having his topcoat made to hug his every contour; in future he would have them a comfortable size, one that did not require any assistance to put on or off.

He had had plenty of time to read the documents his father had given him before he'd left. Not only did he have this house and its fifty acres of parkland, but there were also several farms and a smaller estate in the adjoining county, Norfolk. From what he could ascertain from the figures, the income from these properties was substantial, more than enough to live in style. The tenant who had lived here had let the place become derelict — but why should he spend his own money to repair a house that did not belong to him?

He slicked back his hair with water, checked his boots were polished to a high shine, and was ready to find himself some breakfast. There was a small flock of laying hens in one of the barns, so he would have an omelette.

This was something he had learnt to do when up at Oxford. Eggs without bread or bacon were not his favourite repast, but would do for now.

The Bradshaws must employ a cook — it would make sense for him to move in with them until this house was ready for them all. Once the idea was in his head, he had to act on it. He flung his few garments into his bag and strode out to the stables. The coachman who had come with the carriage soon had the two sturdy horses harnessed and ready.

'I'm going to be living elsewhere until this house is habitable. I think you would be wise to join me.'

The man touched his cap with his whip. 'Thank you, sir. The room above the stables will do if it don't rain, if you get my meaning.'

The carriage arrived at Ravenswood Lodge just as the clock on the church struck eight. God's teeth! What was he thinking? To arrive at such an early time was the height of bad manners. Then he laughed. He was supposed to be a young man ignorant of the ways of society, and this would just confirm his poor credentials.

★   ★   ★

Penny was just completing her morning ablutions when she saw the carriage turn into the short drive. There was only one person who could be visiting at this ungodly hour — it was Mr Trevelyan. What had brought him here?

There was no time for her to dress her hair. She quickly tied it back with a ribbon, pushed her bare feet into her slippers, and thanked the powers that be that she had put on one of her pretty gowns that morning.

Mrs Turner, the cook, and her two daughters, who served as maids-of-all-work, had been up since six o'clock preparing the bread and other things that needed doing. She would insist that these three accompanied them when they moved, as they had proved invaluable these past months.

There was just time for her to put her head around the kitchen door. 'We have an early visitor. Could you serve something tasty in the dining room as soon as possible?'

She then flew back to the vestibule and was just in time to open the door. Foster would be confined to his bed for some time, so they must fend for themselves until he was back on his feet again.

'Good morning, Mr Trevelyan. I thought the arrangement was that I should come to you at ten o'clock, but I must have mistaken the matter as here you are.'

He was not at all put out by her comment. '*Mea culpa*, my dear. I have nothing to eat at my house, so I thought I would come here for my breakfast. I hope that is agreeable to you?'

'As it happens, Edward, my mother is indisposed — no, genuinely so — and my sisters never rise at this hour.' She closed the door behind him and noticed he had a travelling bag in his hand. So startled was she by this observation that she stepped back and put her foot through the hem of her gown.

She lost her balance and would have crashed painfully to the boards if he had not reacted instantly to save her. 'Take care — you almost fell.'

'I am well aware of that, sir. There is no need to point out the obvious.' Flustered by his proximity, she blurted out what she had been thinking instead of keeping it to herself. 'Why have you brought your belongings with you?'

Instead of being offended or embarrassed by her abrupt question, he laughed out loud. 'This house is in a poor state, but at least it is weatherproof and you have a cook. I've not eaten anything but eggs these past days.'

'Then you are most welcome to move in with us, Edward. If you would care to follow me, breakfast is being served in the dining room. You will be relieved to know it is not eggs today.'

He was walking by her side, but she was acutely conscious of the fact that her hem was trailing where she had trodden on it. She would settle him down with his food and then excuse herself and change into something else.

'I'm sorry about your gown, my dear; but even damaged as it is, I much prefer it to the one you were wearing yesterday. Might I also be permitted to say that wearing your hair loose is most attractive?'

The colour was creeping up from her toes to her crown. 'You may not say so, sir. My appearance is none of your concern. If this arrangement is to be successful, then it must be considered as business and not personal.'

'In which case, Miss Bradshaw, from this point on we must resume formalities.'

There was a tempting array of dishes on the sideboard, far more than was usually offered at breakfast, and she could not help but smile when she saw in pride of place a dish of coddled eggs.

'Mr Trevelyan, it is my turn to apologise. I promised there would be none of these presented today.'

His smile was genuine. He was obviously not a man who held grudges. 'Forgive me, but I am ravenous. I care not what it is as long as there is bread to go with it.'

The room was silent, apart from the noise of chewing and his sighs of enjoyment whilst he sated his appetite. He reminded her of her brother, who had also enjoyed his food. Her eyes filled and she blinked furiously. Papa and Ben were gone forever, and she must stop grieving for them both.

'My lord, might we talk in confidence?' Addressing him by his correct title caused him to put down his cutlery, swallow his mouthful and stare at her. His eyes were narrow, his expression hard.

'Go on. I am listening.'

'I should not have poked my nose where it is not wanted, but I could not commit my family to a venture without being sure they would be safe.' She now had his full attention, and he looked less formidable. 'You could have been fleeing from something unsavoury, something that would cause hurt to my sisters. I had to know.'

'You do not think killing a man in a duel unsavoury?'

'I do not approve of such practices, but both parties are aware what they are doing and willingly take that risk. I understand why you must remain incognito, sir, and you have my solemn promise your secret will never be revealed by me.'

'How did I give myself away?'

'I am a keen observer of human behaviour. I can assure you that no one else would have noticed your one mistake. You behaved as a member of the *ton* when you greeted us, and that immediately alerted me.'

'I am dismayed that you discovered my identity so easily. I think I must tell you the whole.'

When he had finished, she was

bothered by his account. 'I take your word for it, sir, that you are an excellent shot. Therefore, there must have been a fault with the weapon used — there can be no other explanation for how a bullet that should have grazed an arm hit your opponent in the chest. The fact that your families have been feuding for generations could mean that there was something untoward going on.'

'Tarnation take it! I should have thought of that myself. I have the actual weapon in the bottom of my bag. I shall examine it later.'

'To return to your former point about being worried your deception will be discovered, I think you need not concern yourself. The newspaper report stated you had left the country with your valet, so neither the family nor the authorities will be looking for you. Why should they associate Mr Edward Trevelyan of Ravenswood Hall with the fugitive Lord Edward Stonham?'

He returned to demolishing his enormous plate of food. When he finally dropped his cutlery, she was on her third cup of tea.

'If you are to reside with us until the house is ready, Mr Trevelyan, then could I ask you to contribute to the housekeeping? I'm sure you would not enjoy eating the way we usually do.'

'I have gold in my bag. I shall give it to you. Shall we continue our business discussion here, or is there somewhere more suitable we can talk without being interrupted?'

'I use the study. There are several things I shall suggest to you. Would you like me to write them down, or do you have a retentive memory?'

'I'm quite capable of making my own list, if you have the necessary pen and paper.'

As she led him briskly to the study, she rehearsed in her head what she wanted to get straight. If she continued to address him formally, that would be one problem solved. She didn't want Mama deciding he would make her a perfect husband. He was not in a position to marry anyone, as by doing so he would either reveal his true identity, or be obliged to marry under a false name. Doing the latter would make the licence invalid, and she was sure he would never subject any young lady to such a thing.

She pushed the freshly trimmed pen and inkpot across the desk to him. The paper was within his arm's reach. There was no necessity for her to write anything down as it was engraved in her memory.

He smoothed the paper, dipped in the pen, and raised one eyebrow expectantly.

'Number one — I would like your permission to appoint a lady's maid for my mother. She is not used to doing for herself. Number two — '

'This is quite ridiculous, you know, my dear. I should have made myself clear. I have sufficient funds for you to appoint a dozen maids if that's what you need to do. I'm hoping you will begin the task of assembling the staff that I shall need to run my establishment. I also need more labourers to get the work completed speedily.' He pushed the paper aside and folded his arms.

'I have your permission to spend what I think is appropriate on anything I think we need?'

'Exactly so.' He looked around the room and shook his head. 'This place could be made more habitable if it was cleaned thoroughly. Appoint as many extra people as you think fit. Where will you find the servants that we require?'

'I can appoint all we need for this house locally. I'm sure you are aware that countryfolk are suffering from the Corn Laws, and there are many veterans of the recent war who have returned and are unable to find employment. These will make the nucleus of the staff you will need to run your house, but the rest must come through an agency in Ipswich.'

'I take it this is a company that your family used?'

'Indeed it was. Will you be setting up your stables? There is a small stud no more than half an hour's drive from here that I can recommend.'

'I take it that you and your sisters will require mounts? I shall also purchase a gig for Lady Bradshaw and a pony cart for the use of the housekeeper.'

'We must be careful not to draw attention to ourselves. There is no necessity to do more than buy one horse, which we will share. Mama can use your carriage if she wishes to make morning calls. Conspicuous expenditure is not a good idea in my opinion.'

His expression changed. For a second she wished the words unspoken. Then she straightened her back and stared right back. She was not going to apologise for saying what needed to be said. If he didn't wish to be unmasked, then he must learn to behave like a country gentleman, not a toplofty London aristocrat.

★　★　★

Edward had been about to put her straight, but she glared at him. He was unused to being gainsaid, especially by a woman. Jemima wouldn't have dared to speak to him like that.

'I shall be guided by your common sense, Miss Bradshaw. If you would be kind enough to direct me to the chamber I shall be occupying for the next few weeks, I shall see myself settled, and then drive over to the stud you mentioned and find myself a horse.'

'I doubt that your coachman would be able to find it without help, sir.'

He swallowed his irritation. 'Then I shall get the directions before I leave. Excuse me, Miss Bradshaw; I will not detain you longer. I'm sure you have domestic duties to attend to.'

She smiled sweetly, but he wasn't fooled for a minute. She then curtsied. 'Indeed I have. There are floors to be scrubbed and potatoes to be peeled, so I must not dally here a moment longer.'

Before he could reply in kind, she was gone. There was no doubting who had got the better of that encounter. If she was not to run him ragged, he would have to sharpen his game.

When he returned to the central hall, there was a diminutive maid hovering nervously at the bottom of the stairs. 'If you would care to follow me, sir, I am to show you to your chamber.'

The child — for she was little more than that — had made no attempt to pick up his bag, and for that he was glad. She could not fail to note the weight and possibly mention it elsewhere. Clothes and personal necessities should not weigh as much as these apparently did.

'Thank you, but there is no need for you to come up. Just tell me which door and I can find it for myself.'

'It's the one at the end of the passageway. It overlooks the garden.' She bobbed, and with a whisk of her skirt returned to her duties elsewhere.

Her directions had been somewhat cryptic, as she had neglected to say at which end of the passageway. When he reached the head of the stairs, he discovered that this stretched in both directions. A pretty oriel window overlooked the drive. From here he could not see the garden. If his calculations were correct, then the chamber at the right would overlook the stables and outbuildings. Therefore, his bedchamber must be to the left.

He was about to push open the door, but then thought he had better not in case his calculations had been incorrect. He was waiting to see if there was an answer when the door beside him flew open and he found himself face to face with the younger Bradshaw sister.

'Why are you knocking on Penny's door?'

'I was told the room I am to occupy was at the end of the corridor, but not which end. So I am trying this one first.'

The girl's belligerent expression turned to a sunny smile. 'This end is for family; the other is guest rooms. Although you are the first person to stay here since we moved last year.'

The door closed, and he strode to the other end of the house and pushed open the door of the room she had indicated. He had expected it to be shrouded in holland covers, neglected, dusty; but the furniture was polished, the bed made up with fresh linen, and there was even a jug of water on the washstand.

This was a great improvement on the rooms he had been occupying. There was a large closet and a dressing room, but no separate parlour. It took him barely five minutes to stow away his garments, and then he had to decide where to hide the bag with the pistol.

Before he put it under the loose floorboard in the dressing room, he would look at it more closely. He sniffed; it smelt, as he'd expected, of gunpowder. Then he peered down the barrel to see if there was anything strange about its construction, but that too was no different from any other pistol he had seen. He rewrapped it in a rag and put it in its hiding place.

He had been foolish to bring it with him, and indeed to keep it at all. The monogram on the stock would immediately identify it as belonging to the Bentley family. There was only one way he could have it in his possession.

Satisfied not even the most diligent of chambermaids would discover the weapon now, he was ready to return to his carriage and go in search of a decent hack.

He paused to examine the view from his window — it did indeed look over a garden, but it was a kitchen garden and not one filled with flowers and roses. As he watched, a familiar figure emerged with a basket over her arm and appeared to be picking some sort of leaf vegetable. His knowledge of horticulture was abysmal, and he had no notion what might be available to harvest so early in the season.

His carriage was facing in the correct direction and the coachman was standing by the team. 'It ain't far, sir, to the stud. I'll find it right enough. I reckon you'll be riding something back and not travelling with me.'

This was the longest sentence the man had spoken since he'd made his acquaintance a week ago. 'I hope so, Travers.'

'If that be the case, sir, Miss Bradshaw has asked me to go into the village and pick up some provisions. Will that be acceptable?'

'It will. Even if I don't purchase a mount, we shall still go and collect whatever Miss Bradshaw requires.'

He jumped into the carriage, not bothering to lower the step, and it rocked violently as Travers resumed his position on the box. With the windows lowered, he was able to inhale the fresh country air and take stock of what was now his land and responsibility.

Papa was in his prime and ran the family estates without the necessity to call on him for assistance. This would be the first time he had been responsible for anything, and he was invigorated by the challenge.

What he didn't know he would soon learn. Ravenswood would be restored and profitable within the year if he had anything to say about it.

4

Once she had collected a basket filled with sufficient salad leaves to accompany cold cuts and potatoes for luncheon, Penny left them in the kitchen. She then went to speak to her sisters, who were now eating a leisurely breakfast themselves. Mama was going to remain in bed this morning, and had only required tea and toast.

'I have several errands to run — will you two come with me, or do you intend to remain here?'

'It rather depends on where you are going and what you intend to do when you get there,' Mattie said as she finished her mouthful.

'I'm going to call on several villagers and begin the task of collecting servants for Mr Trevelyan and ourselves. He has given me permission to appoint as many as I desire, and we are to have personal maids to take care of us again.'

This had their full attention. 'Are you thinking of the Brown family that arrived recently? There are at least four daughters and two sons. They are struggling to survive since their father lost his life fighting for king and country.'

'They are first on my list. I have spoken to Mrs Brown at church, and they are all well-spoken and polite. Mr Brown was not an officer, but a sergeant, and they travelled about with him all over the continent. The older girls would make ideal dressers for us, and we can practice our French with them because I know that they are all fluent in that language, having spent so much time there.'

Beth was already on her feet and shaking out her gown. 'We already have on our boots, and there is no necessity to take a wrap as the weather is clement. We can leave with you immediately.'

As expected, the thought of being

able to offer employment to the Brown family was enough to get her sisters moving. They were like dear Mama in character and looks, whereas she and her brother had taken after their father.

The village was no more than half a mile away, and the Browns occupied a house on the outskirts. The man who had previously owned the property had been derelict in his duties, and she could only presume that he had been as ancient and out of sorts as the old gentleman who had been his tenant at Ravenswood.

All this was going to change if she had anything to do with it. The cottages in the village would be repaired, the occupants offered employment, and the entire neighbourhood would benefit from the arrival of Mr Trevelyan. She had decided it would be better to think of him always by that name to avoid any possible slips when talking about him to others.

'I can hear the boys playing in the garden — would you like to find them whilst I speak to Mrs Brown?'

Her sisters needed no further urging and hurried in the direction of the children's laughter. The front door opened as she arrived, and Mrs Brown greeted her with a curtsy.

'Come in, my dear Miss Bradshaw. Your visits are always welcome here.'

'Thank you, Mrs Brown. I have come with the most excellent news.'

When Penny left the cottage, she had the satisfaction of knowing that not only did they have personal maids for themselves, but they also had restored the fortunes of the Brown family. The three Brown girls were already packing their meagre belongings and would be setting off for Ravenswood Lodge immediately.

Mrs Brown was to take the role of housekeeper; and the two boys, who were ten and twelve years of age, were to work as stable boys as they preferred to be outside. They would not be needed until Ravenswood itself was ready for occupation.

After visiting two other residences, she had the services of two chambermaids and a valet for Edward. Frobisher had been an orderly for an officer, so would be ideal in that position. The fact that he was lame made no difference, as he did not have to run about the place as an outdoor man might have to.

There were no shops in the village — it did not warrant such luxuries — so everything that couldn't be grown or made in the vicinity had to be sent for from Ipswich. She had written a comprehensive list of her requirements and handed it to the coach driver before he left for the stud. Hopefully he would return with what she needed later that day, as the town was only five miles from Nettlested and two miles from the stud.

Mama had risen from her bed of sickness, and instead of being ensconced on the daybed, as was her wont, she was bustling about the place like a woman possessed.

'There you are, Penelope. I cannot

tell you how excited I am. I have set Lily and Daisy scrubbing the rooms in the attic so they are ready for the extra staff when they arrive.'

'I did not expect you to be up, Mama. Are you feeling well enough to be rushing about?'

'I'm perfectly well, thank you, my dear. I have left far too much to you over these past years and it is high time that I took control of the household. You should be thinking about a husband for yourself, and not running this establishment or any other for me and your sisters.'

'I have been happy to do it, and would be bored sitting about the place doing embroidery or reading the latest romantic novel. Mr Trevelyan asked me to take charge of things, and it is on that understanding that we are moving to Ravenswood when it is finished.'

'That was before; things are different now. Before, I was unwell, and now I am not.'

Penny was tempted to take her at her

word and relinquish control, but she knew her mother would find it all too taxing and return to her indolent ways.

'In which case, Mama, you must explain it to Mr Trevelyan when he returns. If he agrees, then of course as a dutiful daughter, I shall stand aside and let you take the reins.'

Her mother looked less enthusiastic. 'Perhaps it would be best if you carried on, as he asked you to do it. Just remember that I am ready to help in any way I can.'

'I am relying on you to instruct the new dressers in their roles when they arrive. They should be here at any moment. Forgive me, Mama; I must go and speak to Cook and arrange for two chickens to be killed for dinner tonight.'

★ ★ ★

Edward was impressed by the small stud he had been sent to, and was able to purchase two horses for himself and a pretty grey mare for the girls. They came with tack and had all been shod recently. The fact that this small horse-breeding concern was on his land, and renting the fields and properties from himself, was probably the reason he got such an excellent deal.

'Travers, what are the stables like at the lodge?' he asked the coachman who had accompanied him on his search, him being a knowledgeable fellow.

'They'll do, sir, but we need more bedding and feed. I'll arrange for these other two to be brought back. If you don't require me anymore, sir, I'll be on me way. I've got errands to run for Miss Bradshaw.'

'I'm going to visit two of my farms, and I shall arrange for the necessary hay, straw and feed to be delivered this afternoon. Please feel free to depart whenever you wish; I do not want to stand in your way.' His sarcasm was lost on the coachman, who smiled happily and walked away whistling to himself.

The gelding he was going to ride

today was a true bay, a rich dark chestnut with black mane and tail. He stood around sixteen hands high and was well up to his considerable weight.

'Bruno's not got the best of tempers, sir, but I reckon you'll have no trouble with him,' the stud owner told him.

'When will the other two be delivered?'

'First thing tomorrow, Mr Trevelyan. I'll ride the black and lead the grey.'

'Excellent. We should have everything in place by then.'

The horses he'd purchased were ideal: handsome, but not smart enough to turn heads and draw attention to themselves. Penny had been correct to remind him about not trying to live like a lord. If he wanted to remain in this neighbourhood without being recognised, it was essential he didn't attract unnecessary gossip.

That said, it would be beholden upon him to entertain once he was at Ravenswood. He had offered to home the Bradshaws on an impulse, but the more he thought about it, the better the plan seemed. They were one of the best families in the area, and it made sense for them to introduce him into local society.

He must discover the whereabouts of a reputable tailor and get his new wardrobe made. He could not make his debut dressed as he was. He had always rather envied his acquaintances; he had no close friends apart from Richard, who had more striking looks than him. Now he was glad his hair was only moderately fair and his features no more than regular. It was less likely he would be recognised than if he was a veritable Adonis.

It had been a wrench to leave Richard uninformed of his true destination. His friend would genuinely believe he and his valet had fled the country. In fact, nobody apart from his father was aware of his new identity. His lips curved. No, that was not true, as Miss Bradshaw was also privy to his secret.

He clicked his tongue and squeezed

with his calves, and Bruno moved forward smoothly. The horse might have a reputation for biting and kicking, but so far he'd proved perfectly amiable. From the deeds and plans he'd been able to study his demesne, which stretched for three miles in all directions, with Ravenswood Hall in the centre.

Nettlested village was only one of three he owned, although the other two were more hamlets than villages. His intention was to visit as many of his tenants as he could today. From what he could understand of the matter, no rents had been paid for the past seven years. He wasn't going to demand they pay the arrears; instead, he would raise the amount and expect it to be paid on the next quarter day.

There had been no estate manager employed since this date, which was no doubt the reason no rents had been collected. One must assume that the farmers concerned would not be overly delighted to see him, as they had had seven years of unexpected extra income.

The first visited was in excellent repair, the farmer's wife polite and apologetic. 'You see, Mr Trevelyan, we had no notion where to pay our dues. We have been putting them aside each year and can bring them to you directly.'

'Mrs Turner, there's no need. Consider it a gift from the estate. I should like to see Mr Turner on quarter day with the new amount.' He had also ordered all the fodder and bedding he required for his new horses, and the good lady had promised it would be brought to him that afternoon without fail.

As he was about to mount and leave the yard, the farmer arrived. He was red in the face and had obviously run from wherever he had been working. 'Would you spare me a few minutes of your time, Mr Trevelyan? There's something you should know before you venture to visit Brook Farm and Eastwick.'

Edward patted Bruno's neck. 'Be patient, my boy. We shall be going soon.' He nodded at his tenant to indicate he was listening.

'It's like this, sir — they won't be best pleased to have to pay their dues in future. They be in cahoots and have spent your rent money on loose women and wine. You'll not find the farms in good repair, nor the land in good heart. Since the estate manager died nigh on seven years ago, they've not bothered to do nothing.'

'Thank you for warning me, Mr Turner. Both shall be evicted forthwith. I'll not visit either place unaccompanied. When I've got half a dozen stout men at my back, I think there will be no argument and they will leave.' He swung into the saddle and gathered the reins. 'Would you be prepared to take on both places?'

The man beamed and nodded. 'That I would, sir, that I would. Our fields adjoin and it will be a simple business to combine all three.'

'I shall get my lawyer to draw up a new tenancy agreement. Mrs Turner informs me you have put aside my rent money for the past few years. Use this money to assist you in this new endeavour.'

The farmer was so pleased that he was hopping from foot to foot like a small child. His head was bobbing up and down, and he appeared for the moment lost for words. Edward didn't wait for him to recover his voice, but raised his hand in farewell and guided his gelding from the immaculate farm-yard.

He turned his mount into a field and gave him his head. The animal had a long stride, didn't fight for the bit, and was in every way exactly what he wanted in a horse. He pulled gently on the reins and got an immediate response. He intended to return with Bruno cool; otherwise he would be obliged to walk about with the gelding himself when he got back, for as yet he had no grooms to take care of the stable yard.

To his astonishment, his arrival was

greeted by two urchins. 'I'm Tom, and this is my little brother Dick, Mr Trevelyan sir. Miss Bradshaw has taken us on to work in the stables.'

He dismounted but did not immediately hand over the reins. If Bruno was vicious, he did not intend that these two be savaged.

'He is a grand big horse, ain't you, fella?' Tom said and deftly removed the reins from Edward's hand. 'You come along with us; we'll make you right comfortable.'

The large gelding flicked his ears back and forth, and for a moment the matter hung in the balance. Then he lowered his head and nudged the boy, who laughed and flung his arm around the animal's neck.

Edward watched them go, and all three seemed remarkably content with the arrangement. Satisfied Bruno wasn't going to bite or kick either of the lads, he strode into the house. The front door seemed to be permanently open — something he wasn't sanguine about.

This reminded him about the ancient butler who had collapsed and been taken to the downstairs apartment. The house was noisy today. He could hear the sounds of girls scrubbing upstairs, and the two boys seemed happy in their employment.

In his previous existence, he had never noticed the menials going about their jobs. Knew none of their names and cared little about their well-being as long as he was served efficiently. Things were different here, and he rather liked the change. Papa would disapprove of such familiarity with the staff; but for the first time in his life, Edward could do as he damned well pleased.

★   ★   ★

Penny had barely had time to snatch a mouthful of food since she'd broken her fast with Edward. Appetising aromas drifted through the house from the kitchen and her mouth watered. Dinner was served at four o'clock regardless of the season, so she only had two hours to wait, and she doubted she would faint from hunger before then.

She was used to being on short commons; the rest of the family always got fed first when there was little to eat during the long winter months. No doubt this was why there was little discernible difference between her back view and her front.

Mattie and Beth had joined Mama in the garden, where they were sitting in the rose arbour, bereft of blooms at this time of the year, and enjoying the late spring sunshine. She gathered up her skirt and ran lightly up the stairs to investigate how the cleaning was progressing.

The three Brown sisters, although employed as personal maids, had been quite happy to tie sacks around their gowns and help with the spring clean.

'This is looking quite splendid. However, it might be sensible to open a few windows and let the sunshine dry the boards.' One of the girls, Molly, started to scramble to her feet, but Penny waved her back.

'No, I shall do it; you carry on. I would like to get this floor finished so you can start downstairs tomorrow.'

The oriel window didn't open, but there were two at each end of the passageway that did. The ones that lit the family side of the house were often opened, and so moved smoothly enough. However, when Penny attempted to raise the first of the two on the right, it refused to budge.

She was huffing and puffing and muttering under her breath when Edward spoke from behind her. 'Allow me, my dear. This is not a suitable pastime for a gently bred young lady.'

Without a by-your-leave, he put his hands around her waist and lifted her aside as if she weighed no more than a bag of feathers. He then gripped the bottom of the window and heaved. Unfortunately, she had already loosened it, and it flew up so unexpectedly he was thrown backwards.

He ricocheted against the wall and then sat down on his backside with a thud. If she had not laughed, all might have been well. His expression changed from irritated to angry. He was on his feet before she had time to react and was towering over her.

For a second she was terrified, but then common sense took over. His dignity had been dented, and he was furious, but would not harm her; of that she was certain. She remained where she was and did not take a step back from him.

'I beg your pardon for laughing, sir. I did not mean to offend you.'

His expression changed instantly. His smile made her forget the momentary fear. 'And I apologise for my surliness. I'm not accustomed to falling on my derrière.'

She returned his smile. 'At least the window is now open, and you were on your feet so speedily I doubt that the maids were aware of your mishap.'

He looked puzzled. 'Why should I be

bothered what they think? They are here to work, not to form an opinion of their betters.'

They were talking quietly and could not be overheard. 'I disagree, Mr Trevelyan; they have every right to be considered and their feelings taken into account.'

5

The girl was looking at him with disapproval — not something he was accustomed to in his previous life. Jemima had thought him a god among men, and would not have dreamed of disagreeing with his views or taking him to task under any circumstances.

'Then we shall have to accept we have differing views on the subject, Miss Bradshaw. I hope this does not mean there will be friction in our joint household? I insist on my establishment being run smoothly and cannot abide any sort of unpleasantness.'

She nodded politely. 'I understand completely, Mr Trevelyan. No one should be obliged to endure any sort of friction in their home. I can assure you that all the staff I appoint will behave as they should, and I guarantee they will do their job so efficiently you will not be aware of their existence.'

He was about to answer when he happened to glance behind her and saw the three girls with buckets had vanished. They had done so silently. How had Miss Bradshaw managed to convey this instruction without him being aware of it?

'Are there any more windows you would like me to open before I go to my room?'

'Thank you; the one you have done will be sufficient to dry the boards.'

She moved away, and he could not help but be aware that she was displeased with him. For some incomprehensible reason, this state of affairs was not to his liking. There was nothing he could do to rectify things at the moment, but at the earliest opportunity he would do whatever was necessary to bring this fierce young lady onto his side.

He strode into his chamber and found it already occupied. The young man of medium height, smartly dressed — indeed, a deal smarter than himself — bowed. 'Good afternoon, Mr Trevelyan. I am Frobisher, your valet.'

For the first time in his life, Edward was incapable of speech. There was a jug of hot water steaming gently on the washstand, clean towels to one side, and a complete change of garments neatly arranged on the bed. Where the devil had these come from? As they certainly weren't his.

'I see. I take it Miss Bradshaw appointed you?' The man nodded and continued to look him directly in the eye. 'Where did those come from?'

'Miss Bradshaw thought you might like to borrow from Mr Benedict Bradshaw's extensive wardrobe until you have had time to replenish your own. I took the liberty of comparing your items with these, and they will be an excellent fit.'

Edward was about to say he wouldn't wear a dead man's clothes, but thought this would be childish. 'I don't suppose you know where I can get things made?'

'Someone is coming from Ipswich tomorrow to take your measurements. He will be bringing patterns from which you can choose your style and material.'

'Excellent. From your demeanour, I gather you have experience as a gentleman's gentleman?'

Frobisher was already at his side, expertly removing his topcoat and knotting his cravat. 'I was orderly to Colonel Fitzwilliam. I received a bullet in my leg and was unable to continue in the position. However, I don't believe my lameness will affect my ability to take care of you efficiently, sir.'

This man was remarkably garrulous for a servant, and Edward wasn't sure he was quite comfortable with that. He preferred to be served in silence; for whoever was doing the serving to speak only when spoken to.

'I believe I shall be the judge of that, Frobisher. I shall keep you on a month's probation. If I find your services satisfactory, then I shall make the position permanent.'

In no time at all, Edward was clean and freshly garbed in garments that did indeed fit him very well. The gong to remind family members to go up and change for dinner had been sounded whilst he was dressing. He thought he would be downstairs sometime in advance of the ladies. It would give him time to see what improvements had been made.

The house certainly smelt fresh, and there was a liveried footman waiting to open the drawing room door for him. He stopped short in surprise.

'Lady Bradshaw, Miss Bradshaw, Miss Matilda and Miss Elizabeth, I apologise if I am tardy.' He half-bowed and they all curtsied.

'Penny insisted we were here early, Mr Trevelyan, so I can assure you that you are not late. This is the first time we have dressed for dinner, and I own I am feeling happier than I have since my dearest husband and only son perished.'

'I am delighted to hear you say so, ma'am.' He was about to move into his accustomed mode of flattery and charm when Miss Bradshaw cleared her throat. He glanced at her and she shook her head almost imperceptibly. Thank God she was alert. He must remember to behave like a gentleman not used to the social mores.

He smiled at the sisters. 'I'm wearing borrowed clothes. I hope I pass muster. You both look quite splendid.'

Instead of coughing, Penny — he could not continue to be at odds with her and think of her formally — was choking in her handkerchief. Had he overdone it? Perhaps mentioning he was in their dead brother's clothes was doing it too brown.

But it was too late to retract his casual comment. Lady Bradshaw smiled, unbothered by his tactless remark. 'Penelope will not allow dear Ben's belongings to be disposed of, which is fortunate, is it not?'

He nodded solemnly. 'I am most

grateful, my lady. There is to be a person coming tomorrow to start getting my wardrobe in order. I am grateful for the loan of these things until I can appear in new items of my own.'

His rambling was greeted with smiles, and then the new footman announced that dinner was served. Penny drifted up beside him.

'You are impersonating a gentleman inexperienced in the ways of society, not a complete ninny.'

★   ★   ★

She was gone from his side before he could respond, which was probably fortunate, as what he had intended to say could only have exacerbated matters. He was sure she would see that his smile was false if she cared to look in his direction.

The dining room looked splendid. The crisp white damask table covering, the crystalware as good as any he had seen in his own house, and the central flower arrangement were quite stunning. There were three courses each, with several removes, and all as delicious as anything he'd eaten before.

The conversation around the table was lively, and despite his ill humour, he found himself joining in with the laughter and badinage. When Lady Bradshaw put down her cutlery and stood, the girls immediately followed suit.

Penny was watching him to see how he would react. He decided to do what he wanted, which was not to remain here on his own drinking port, but go with the ladies into the drawing room.

'I believe I should stay here, my lady, but I've no intention of doing so. I'm hoping that we can play a hand or two of cards.'

'I do not enjoy playing myself, but my daughters will be happy to do so as long as there is no gambling involved. I do not approve of that.'

'I have never indulged, as I've not

had the wherewithal to do so. We could play whist, as there are four of us. Would that be acceptable, Miss Bradshaw?'

'I shall partner Beth, while you must join Mattie. That way the sides will be equal.'

'You are assuming, Miss Bradshaw, that I am a skilled player.'

'As it was you who suggested we play whist, I hope I am not incorrect in my assumptions.'

'I was funning. I am a competent player of most card games. I have a variation of whist that I think will be more fun and doesn't require a partner.'

Once they were settled around the table, he explained the rules, and all three of them agreed his version of the game was going to be more enjoyable than the standard version. They played and laughed and thoroughly enjoyed themselves until the tea tray was fetched in.

Edward had no liking for this insipid

brew, as he much preferred coffee, so he excused himself and said he was going to check on his new horse. Penny caught him up as he was exiting through a side door that led directly to the stables.

'Mr Trevelyan, I must apologise for my comments earlier. All this must be so difficult for you, and I'm not making it any easier by constantly criticising.'

'Without your sharp eyes, I would make a sad mull of it and be uncovered as an impostor. There is something I should like to ask you. Do you know anything about the tenants of Brook Farm or Eastwick?'

'Not a lot, but they have unsavoury reputations. There has been talk of wild parties and visiting from London for debauchery and suchlike.'

Now was not the time to enquire if she knew of what she spoke or was just repeating what she had been told. A young lady like her should not be aware there was such a thing as debauchery.

'I was told the same by Farmer

Turner. My intention is to evict both of them, but I cannot do so until I have reliable men to accompany me. I doubt they will go quietly.'

'Some of the men I sent to work on Ravenswood Hall were employed there, and they would be the men to ask. I'm sure they would also be only too happy to help you in your task to remove these tenants.' To his surprise, she did not return to the drawing room, but accompanied him outside in the darkness.

'You are not suitably dressed to come to the stables, Miss Bradshaw . . . '

'Oh dear! Am I no longer to be called by my given name? Have I so offended you?'

'You are a baggage, my dear Penny, and it is high time somebody took you in hand.' He heard her sharp intake of breath and laughed. 'Fear not; I have no intention of volunteering for that position. However, I shall do my damnedest to find you a suitable husband as soon as we are all established in my home.'

Her peal of laughter echoed into the night. 'Then you will be disappointed, Edward. I have no intention of relinquishing my freedom for any gentleman. I have been my own mistress for too long. You must confine your attention to finding partners for my sisters if we are not to be at daggers drawn.'

'I suppose that is only to be expected. After all, at two-and-twenty, you must consider yourself at your last prayers.' His tone was light, his remark meant to be taken in jest.

When he received no answer, he looked to his side, but she had gone. Surely she had not taken his words to be sincere? She might not be the woman for him, but she would make somebody a wonderful wife. Hopefully she had found his company irritating and that was why she had left so abruptly. Either explanation did not please him.

His very existence was in the hands

of this young woman, and he would do well to remember that. If his knowledge of the fairer sex was accurate, the description could not be relied upon if they were angry with the person whose secret they were keeping. He doubted that even Jemima could be relied upon in such circumstances.

The stable yard was quiet; *too* quiet. There should be the soft sound of horses munching hay, the clatter of the stable boys cleaning tack somewhere. He should have thought to bring a lantern, as it was now too dark to see anything clearly.

He almost left the ground when someone spoke from behind him. 'The horses are in the paddock, Mr Trevelyan. They will do better there than cooped up in the stables when it is so clement.'

It was one of the stable boys, but he couldn't decide which. 'Thank you for letting me know. There will be two further arriving tomorrow morning. Is everything prepared for them?'

'It is, sir. The feed store is full, the

hay store also. They can be kept inside or out and do well enough.'

'Good night, lad. Make sure that Bruno is saddled and waiting for me at nine o'clock.'

'He will be ready. Good night, master.'

On his return to the house, Edward considered the exchange. He had been brought up never to thank servants; to expect they would do their duty regardless of the circumstances. His new persona had no such scruples, and he was forced to admit that being on more familiar terms with his minions was not as unpleasant as he had been led to believe.

He was not sanguine about Penny's sudden departure. He would check that she had returned safely to join her mother before he retired.

★ ★ ★

Penny didn't return to join her family, as she was too distressed by his casual remark. Did he really consider her to be unmarriageable? She was no beauty, and had no dowry, but she did have intelligence, compassion and wit. These were not required from a wife; in fact, were probably viewed as unfavourable traits.

She must not remain here snivelling in the darkness. She was made of stronger stuff than that and would not let the casual comments of a stranger overset her. She sniffed and wished she had thought to bring her reticule so she had a handkerchief to dry her eyes.

'Here, sweetheart, use this.' The soft square of cotton was pushed into her hand. She took it and scrubbed her eyes, wishing he had not come across her when she was so upset.

'I am a brute to make you cry by my thoughtless words. They were intended to be a joke, my dear. You are a beautiful young woman, and I intend to settle a dowry on you and your sisters. I promise you there will not be a shortage of gentlemen queueing for

your hand once you have been reintro-
duced to society.'

She could just discern his outline in
the darkness and impulsively reached
out and took his hand. 'You must not
do that, Edward, for we are strangers to
you. One day you will have a family of
your own and you must keep your funds
for them, not hand them away to us.'

To her consternation, his hand covered hers. Apart from being touched by
her father and brother, she had never
experienced physical contact with another
gentleman, and it made her head spin.
She wasn't sure if it was shock or excitement that coursed through her.

'Sweetheart, I can never marry as I
cannot use my own name, and any union
contracted as Mr Trevelyan would be
null and void. Therefore, I consider myself
part of the Bradshaw clan and will gain
pleasure from seeing you all happy.'

He showed no sign of removing his
hand from hers, nor did he step away.
His proximity was making her unsettled.
Then he released her and she was able

to breathe easily once more.

'I do not understand why you should wish to do this. We have only been acquainted for a day or so . . . '

'And yet in that time you have unmasked me, and I now owe my very existence to your continued support.'

It was as if someone had tipped a pail of icy water over her head. She finally understood his motivation. What he was doing for her family was to keep himself safe, and no other reason. It was not so romantic as his suggestion that he was looking for a substitute family, but she was a pragmatic young woman and understood exactly why he would think to tie his life to theirs. By doing this, he could be sure she would not reveal what she knew, as this would put her sisters and mother back in penury. Family came first, as it should.

'I have given you my word that your secret will never be revealed by me. And to return to your previous point about you being unable to marry, I disagree. If whoever you marry is not aware of the deception, then how will she or your future progeny suffer? Ignorance is bliss, is it not?'

'I had not thought of it like that. Thank you for giving me some encouragement. I was engaged to the most beautiful and loving young lady, and it has broken my heart to have had to abandon her. I doubt I shall ever find another whom I can love as well, but I hope that one day I might have children of my own.'

'I'm sure that whoever you were betrothed to is equally devastated. I am sorry for your loss. Forgive me, Edward, but I must go in, as my sisters and mother will be wondering what is keeping me.'

'Good night, my dear. I am indebted to you.'

She hurried in, but the heavy evening dew had already soaked through her indoor slippers and wet the hem of her evening gown before she was inside. She viewed the damage with a rueful smile. This would teach her not to venture outside onto the grass but to remain on the paths in future. Indeed, straying from the path was something she was overfond of doing. However attractive their benefactor was, she must not let herself become emotionally entangled with him. There could be no future for them, as he had so clearly pointed out.

6

Edward set out the next morning and was no more than a mile from his present home when he changed his mind about his destination. He would visit the hall and talk to the foreman before he went to see his lawyers. The place was unrecognisable as a dwelling. Everywhere he looked, there were workmen plastering, painting, repairing or polishing.

An urchin had come to hold Bruno, and Edward left his gelding without a second thought. If the beast had been vicious before, he certainly wasn't now. A man of middle years, his face and hair white with dust, approached him.

'Good morning, Mr Trevelyan, sir. I'm Sam Bishop, foreman here. I was going to come and see you today, as there are things I need to know before we can progress.'

'All I want is for the place to be restored to how it should be. Lady Bradshaw and her daughters will be living here and they will be selecting the fabrics, wallpapers and paint colours. When will you be requiring such items?' He smiled in what he hoped was a suitable way for a young gentleman with no knowledge of such things.

'Not for another sennight at least, sir. But, begging your pardon, I don't reckon what you might be needing will come from the warehouses in London that quickly unless you go yourself to order.'

'I'm sure that Lady Bradshaw will be only too happy to travel to town. I shall discuss it with her later today. There is another matter I must speak to you about pertaining to Brook Farm and Eastwick.'

He had the man's full attention now. 'I heard you'll be wanting to evict them varmints from your properties. There's no point in asking my men to do it, sir, as they value their lives and families too highly to take that chance.'

'I see. I shall have to find another way to remove them that doesn't place anybody at risk.'

He reclaimed his horse, swung into the saddle, and resumed his journey to the market town. If his father had known how complicated matters were on this estate, he probably wouldn't have sent him here.

He realised he had left without bothering to inform anyone of his destination. He had also forgotten that the tailor was to come to take his measurements that day. Another thing that belatedly occurred to him was that the stagecoach from London to Norwich stopped in Ipswich and it was always possible there would be a passenger disembarking there who might recognise him. The risk was slight — but he thought it would be wiser to send for his lawyers and not ride there himself.

There was a groom employed to take care of the five horses; he would send him with a letter and request that his legal team came to see him at their earliest convenience. They were not privy to his real identity, of course, but were well aware that he was a wealthy young man and could put a deal of business their way if he so wished. If the unwelcome tenants remained where they were for a week or two longer, so be it. Far better to get the matter dealt with properly than rush into it and cause problems for innocent people.

One of the stable boys appeared as he dismounted and led his horse away. There was bound to be stationery in the library, so he headed in that direction. Penny was there before him, reading a copy of *The Times*. Seeing a young lady with her nose in such a journal gave him pause. He could not quite decide if he was pleasantly surprised or alarmed at such unusual behaviour.

'Good morning, Edward. Did you wish to speak to me about something?'

'I did, but first I would like to borrow some paper and write a letter to my lawyers and also to my bankers.'

She didn't put the paper down, merely waived in the direction of the desk upon which fabrics and furnishing items were kept. Whilst she returned to her reading, he quickly wrote the letter requesting that the lawyer came to see him. He would elaborate on his requirements when the gentleman arrived.

He sanded both papers, folded them neatly into squares and melted the sealing wax. Automatically he went to put his signet ring with the family crest into the molten wax, then saw his naked finger. He looked around and saw the Bradshaw seal and used this instead.

'Do the bells work now?'

She looked up. 'They were always functioning; there was just nobody to respond to the summons. I'm sure someone will come if you ring today.'

The footman arrived promptly and Edward explained his requirements. The young man bowed and took the letters. Edward didn't consider for a minute that these missives would not arrive at their destinations by lunchtime and that replies would not be in his hands that afternoon.

Penny now folded the newspaper carefully and put it aside. She was obviously waiting to hear what he had come in to ask.

'I would like you to go to the warehouses in London for me and select the necessary paint, wallpaper, furnishings and fabrics that will be required.'

'I have no notion how much of anything will be needed, or for that matter, what your taste is as to the colour and pattern.'

He flicked aside his coat-tails and sat opposite. 'I am but a naïve, inexperienced clerk and have no knowledge of such things myself. I shall rely on your excellent discernment.'

Her delighted laughter filled the room. 'That is nonsense, and you know it. Nevertheless, I should be delighted to go. I once visited with my father and believe I could find the best places. Do you have a list of some sort to assist? How many windows need curtains, and of what length and breadth should they be? How many rolls of wallpaper will need to be printed?'

He held up his hands in surrender. 'But as you have surmised, my dear, I'm ignorant of all these facts. Perhaps you would accompany me to the hall sometime today and ascertain for yourself what is required?'

'Have you looked in the attics? Sometimes there are treasures stored up there.'

'Another thing I have been delinquent in doing. Do you wish to explore them when we go?'

'I cannot wait. I shall travel to town by stagecoach, as it passes only a mile from here.'

Only then did he consider the impropriety of asking an unmarried lady to wander around Cheapside without a gentleman in attendance to protect her. He was about to retract his request but then thought better of it.

'That sounds like a sensible idea, but you will travel post, not by the common stage.'

'I shall do no such thing, Edward. It would cost more to do so than we have been living on for an entire year. Remember what I said about extravagance.'

He bit back his sharp retort. She was not his ward, nor indeed a genuine relation, so was free to do as she pleased as long as her own parent agreed. Somehow, he rather thought Lady Bradshaw was in the habit of agreeing to everything her opinionated daughter suggested.

* * *

Penny was so excited she almost hugged him, but wisely restrained. To be going to London at someone else's expense, to be given *carte blanche* to furnish Ravenswood, was more than she could have ever expected. To think that scarcely two weeks ago she had been worrying herself sick about how they were to survive the next winter without a miracle — and then he had arrived with his life-changing suggestion.

She was at the door and then could not leave without expressing her thanks. 'Edward, I know we are benefiting you, but you have literally saved us from destitution. We shall be forever in your debt.'

His smile warmed her to her very core. 'My absolute pleasure, sweetheart. It is a mutually beneficial arrangement, and as such we owe no debt of any sort to each other.'

'I think I just heard a chaise pull up outside. I expect it is the tailor come to take your measurements. Shall we arrange to go to Ravenswood when you have finished?'

He nodded and strode across to join her at the door. 'Let us hope that this tedious business does not take too long.' She raised an eyebrow at his tone and he chuckled. 'Do not fear, I shall be suitably excited about the thought of new garments as befits my lowly station.'

She ran away from him and his laughter followed her. He really was irresistible when he chose to be. She had blithely agreed to go to town on his behalf, but had a feeling her mother might not be so delighted at the prospect.

'I absolutely forbid it, Penelope Bradshaw. What are you thinking? What is he thinking? I suppose the gentleman from a lowly background could not possibly understand that a young lady does not travel the countryside in a common stage, and — '

'Mama, you know there is little point in you telling me I cannot do anything when I have made up my mind I shall do it. It would be even more outrageous if he came with me, don't you think? Of course, dearest Mama, the matter would be solved if you came too.'

'Travel to London? I could not do so. I can feel a palpitation coming on at the very thought. You will do as you think fit, as you always do, and I suppose that in our reduced circumstances there is little need to protect your reputation. After all, two weeks ago you were intending to be a servant yourself.'

'I was indeed, and see how our fortunes have changed? I would not suggest that either Mattie or Beth gallivant around the place unescorted, but as I do not intend to marry, a few dents in my reputation are of little importance to me.'

Her mother's attention was attracted to the sound of another visitor. 'Go and see who is arriving on horseback now.'

There was no need for her to do so, as her sisters burst in. 'A man has come on another huge gelding and is leading the prettiest dapple-grey mare you have ever seen. Do you think that is for us to ride?'

'I believe so, Mattie. Edward promised he would get us a mount we could share.'

Her mother had roused herself sufficiently to come across and see for herself. 'How kind of him, but of course he cannot know that a young lady must not ride alone. I cannot agree to any of you going out unaccompanied.'

'In which case, Mama, we shall have to take it in turns to ride around the paddock. I've no wish to go out without Beth or Penny even with the groom beside me.'

'I think that one of the carriage horses will also go under saddle. Why don't you go and enquire?'

They ran off happily, already deciding who would ride the mare and who the less glamorous chestnut gelding.

'I am going to Ravenswood later, Mama, so that I have the information I need when I visit the warehouses. Why don't you peruse the latest fashion plates and see if there is a particular dress fabric I should look out for?'

The thought of having gowns made up in the latest materials was enough to distract her mother, and no more was said about the inappropriateness of her journey. She had been dwelling on the fact that there was something not quite right about the death of Lord Bentley. She could hardly write to her acquaintances and enquire, as this might well draw attention to Edward. However, whilst she was in the metropolis, she would somehow endeavour to visit the neighbourhood in which the Bentley family resided and make enquiries.

When she was with Edward this afternoon, she would bring up the topic and elicit as much information as she could about this family. The Season would be drawing to a close. The Bentley family would have removed themselves to their country estate after the death of the heir, which would suit her purpose splendidly. There should be a skeleton staff left in residence, and it was to those she would address her enquiries.

Just after noon, she was mounted on the pretty dapple-grey mare, Misty, and Edward was astride his latest purchase. The two horses seemed firm friends already, so there was no necessity to ride apart.

'When do you intend that I go to London?'

'As soon as I have a banker's draft in my hand, you can go. I shall also ensure you have sufficient flimsies and coins for incidental purchases. Lady Bradshaw was remarkably sanguine about your proposed excursion.'

'I promised I would purchase her some of the Indian cottons that are so fashionable at the moment. I also suggested that she accompany me, and the two things were enough to persuade her I should be perfectly safe to go on my own.' She saw his frown and hastily added, 'I shall have a manservant and my maid travelling with me, so there's no need to look so cross.'

'I am still uncomfortable with the fact that you are so careless of your reputation. What if you are seen by acquaintances? Would not your sisters suffer if you were considered beyond the pale?'

'No; it might be considered out of the ordinary for me to go on my own, but in the unlikely event that I do meet anyone I know, they will be well aware of my circumstances and that there are in fact no gentlemen in my family who could have come with me.'

'What about the person who inherited the title and the properties? Is he not now head of the household, and are not your sisters his wards?'

'Indeed, if he was a gentleman that would be the case, and we would not be living where we are. The man is so distant a relation he can hardly be called one at all. He has half a dozen children of his own and had no interest in adding us to his household. We were given instructions to be gone before they arrived and barely had time to pack and find ourselves another home.'

'I should be appalled at his callousness, but in fact I am delighted he behaved so badly. If he hadn't, then you would not be here, and I would not be riding beside you.'

For a moment she thought he was joking, but then saw the sincerity in his expression. 'The only fly in the ointment, as far as I'm concerned, is that the Bradshaw title and estates are in the hands of a totally unsuitable person. I shudder to think what is happening to our people, as I am quite certain he will not take care of them as we did.'

This was the ideal opportunity to ask him questions about his family. 'Are you the only child?'

'Unfortunately, that is true. If there were others, then it would be easier for my father to bear the separation. My mother died in childbirth when I was still in leading strings. He never married again.'

'If you do not mind me asking, why would the Bentley family intend to do you harm?'

He gave her a brief explanation and she was mystified. 'It seems inexplicable to me that this should be continued to the present day. One would expect such behaviour several hundred years ago, not in a modern society like ours.'

'Exactly so. The continuance is not on our side, I can assure you. Why do you ask?'

'Curiosity, no more than that. The fact that Lord Bentley deliberately goaded you into fighting him needs further investigation. If he intended to do you harm, then why didn't he shoot you when he had the chance?'

'I have thought about that myself. He should have selected foils, as I am no swordsman and he is renowned for his ability with the blade; yet he selected pistols, in which I am an expert.'

'It makes no sense. Why would he risk his own life if what he wanted was to murder you?'

He shook his head. 'It is a conundrum, Penny, but one you must not concern yourself with. I am resigned — no, happy with my new situation. If it wasn't for the fact that I can never see my parent again, I am forced to admit that I much prefer my new life to my old.'

'Are the Bentley family wealthy? Do

they reside in a prestigious part of town?'

'They have a house in Hanover Square. Enough of this conversation, sweetheart. I have put it behind me and you must do the same.'

They were now turning into the drive of Ravenswood Hall and immediately she saw the difference. The weeds had been cleared, the grass cut and the trees pruned. There were no longer holes in the roof, and all windows were sound. The place was swarming with workmen: carpenters, plasterers, and labourers of every type were busy setting things to rights.

One of the gardeners put down his rake and came to take the horses. 'We shall not be above an hour.'

He offered his arm and she slipped her hand through it. Only as she was ascending the stairs at his side did it occur to her this might give a completely erroneous impression to any of the numerous men who were watching wide-eyed.

'This is quite unsuitable. Going in like this makes me look like the lady of the manor.' She tried to pull a hand away, but his other hand came around and held it fast.

'I've told you before, my dear, it is of no interest to me what my servants think.'

Unless she wanted to create an unpleasant scene, she had no option but to remain at his side. He released her once they were in the central hall. This appeared to be almost ready for painting. The black and white tiled floor was pristine, and the magnificent carved oak staircase that dominated the space was repaired and polished.

She forgot her momentary annoyance with her companion and turned slowly to admire what had been accomplished. 'This is indeed a splendid hall. It needs nothing else but a coat of whitewash to be complete. With the addition of a sideboard, a few small tables, some paintings and a mirror or two, it will be perfect.'

'Do you have any family portraits we could hang? Obviously I have none.'

'We could bring nothing of value with us. Everything pertaining to my family is in Bradshaw Manor. The only good thing about that situation is that the entire estate and contents of the houses are entailed and cannot be disposed of.'

'I assume he is a Bradshaw?'

'The family have that name, but as I said before, the connection to our family is so tenuous as to be almost nonexistent. Heaven knows where the lawyers found them.' She gathered her skirts in one hand and headed for the stairs. 'I shall now explore the attics. Are you coming with me, sir?'

7

Edward hurried after her. Not because he had any real desire to visit the attics, but because he was enjoying her company too much to let her go alone. She flew up the stairs in front of him, revealing her riding boots beneath her habit. Such a voluminous garment was not ideal for rummaging about in attics, but at least she was not showing any of her more interesting assets. A surge of desire ripped through him as he imagined what she might look like unclothed. Perhaps spending time unchaperoned in the attics with Penny was not such a good idea after all.

How she found her way so easily in a house she'd never visited, he had no notion; but she was along two passageways, up a second flight to the nursery floor, and then finally paused for breath at the door that led to the third floor.

'We will need illumination even though it's light. Attics are notoriously dark and filled with cobwebs.'

'Wait here; I'll have a servant fetch some candles.'

'There are no bells to ring up here, Edward. It will be quicker to fetch them yourself.'

He grinned. 'I have a better idea.' He strode to the nursery stairs and yelled for someone to bring candles. His voice echoed down the empty stairwell and immediately elicited a robust reply.

'I'll bring you some, sir. There's plenty in the bedchambers.'

He turned to find her giggling into her handkerchief and unable to speak.

'I know — shocking behaviour! But it worked, didn't it?'

She spluttered and wiped her eyes before answering. 'I thought you a serious gentleman, but now you have shown your true colours. You are as outrageous as I.'

Her comment pleased him. 'If I had shouted like that when I was a boy, I would have been thrashed. I was obliged to conform to my father's expectations and long ago learned to control any thoughts of silliness.'

'Good grief! Are you telling me that from this point on you are going to behave as a madman?'

There was thunder of hobnailed boots on the stairs, and a beaming workman arrived with two candlesticks and four candles. He had also had the foresight to bring a tinderbox.

'Here you are, master, missus. You'll need them in those attics.'

The items were handed over and the man departed as nosily as he had come. His companion was no longer laughing. She had been right to be worried about them wandering about the house together. Servants gossiped, and what had transpired here would be common knowledge by tomorrow. He was about to beg her pardon when yet again she surprised him.

'I hope you don't object to having your name linked to mine? Nothing we can do about it now. Shall we go and investigate upstairs?'

The door was stiff, and he had to apply all his considerable weight to it in order to get it open. 'I doubt anyone has been up here for years. Are you quite sure you wish to proceed? There will be rodents and spiders galore.'

'I am not overfond of mice and rats but have no objection to spiders. You may go first, and hopefully any four-legged creatures lurking near the door will hide before I get there.'

She expertly used the tinderbox, and soon both candles were alight. He tucked the spares into his jacket pocket. She held one and he the other. He viewed the narrow staircase with disfavour. 'It's extremely dirty. Your pretty gown will be ruined up here.'

'As I am to have a new wardrobe at your expense, that hardly matters.'

Her causal comment caused him to trip over the second step and drop the candlestick. 'God damn it to hell.'

His language didn't shock her but

made her laugh. 'Allow me to relight your candle, Edward. I can see you are not only mad but also clumsy and inclined to swear.'

This was the outside of enough. He reached behind her and yanked the door shut. Two could play this teasing game. He stepped close so they were scarcely an inch apart. She was pressed hard against the closed door, and from the quivering of the candle flame her hand was shaking.

Immediately he regretted his actions, and was preparing to step away and apologise when he realised she wasn't frightened, but laughing. He had always hated being a figure of fun. He forgot who he was, who she was, and gave in to his desire.

He picked her up and crushed her against his chest. Her feet were in mid-air, her heat making him lose all common sense. He tilted her head and he was lowering his mouth to kiss her when she spoke softly.

'Edward, if you do this you will have

crossed the line. Are you willing to take such a risk?'

'Are you?'

Her arms encircled his neck and her fingers buried themselves in his hair. He had his answer. Her lips were sweeter than any he had kissed, and as they softened beneath his, he wanted nothing more than to take what she was freely giving.

★ ★ ★

Penny wanted the kiss to go on forever. She had never experienced anything so heady, so exciting. Then he gently disentangled her and replaced her on her feet. He didn't apologise and she was glad of that.

'This is a dangerous game we're playing, sweetheart, and I don't think that you quite understand the rules. Come, let us go and investigate up there before anything else untoward occurs.'

It took her a few moments to recover her composure. Her candle had gone out during the embrace, but he had no difficulty using the tinderbox and getting both of them burning again.

'I'm not sure if we should apologise to each other for breaking all the rules. I am not sorry; I really enjoyed the experience.'

He had his back to her and didn't turn as he spoke. 'You are an innocent; I am not. I'm not in the habit of seducing young ladies and do not intend to start now. I too enjoyed our kiss, but it will not be repeated. In future I shall treat you as my sister.'

For some reason this didn't upset her, but annoyed her. She took the two steps necessary to bring her up behind him and then poked him sharply in the back. 'Don't stand there dithering. Get a move on. I have not got all day to waste looking in your attics.'

It had the desired effect, and he surged up the remaining stairs and kicked open the door at the top. There was an ominous scuttling and then silence. He moved away from the door, and immediately she could see almost well enough to dispense with her candle. There were windows at either end of the space, and if they had not been so grimy, the area would have been flooded with sunlight.

In the few minutes she had had to gather her thoughts, Penny had decided she was going to pretend they had never kissed or exchanged heated words. She would treat him as she had always done and trust that he would respond in kind. She had no intention of being spoken to as he did to her younger sisters — she was a woman grown and would not be treated like a schoolroom miss.

He placed his candle on what looked like an oak sideboard, then pulled out his handkerchief and walked to the window and began to clean it. She had nothing to use unless she tore off a strip of petticoat, and she decided to do that. He had called her ensemble pretty, but in fact it was an old gown, and her underpinnings were patched and worn.

She hurried to the far end of the

attic, reached down and ripped a large chunk from her petticoat. The sound was hideously loud in the silence. She had not thought this through.

'What in the name of Hades are you doing now?' He had turned and was staring at her as if she was fit for Bedlam. The way they had behaved this afternoon, they could both be considered candidates for a lunatic asylum.

'I have no handkerchief about my person, Mr Trevelyan, so I'm using what is available. Kindly get on with what you're doing and allow me to do the same.'

He made a noise something between a growl and a cough but did as she requested. By the time they had both completed their tasks, there was no need for the candles.

'I can't believe it. This must be the furniture that was originally downstairs. Your distant relative must have had it stored here when he rented the property out.'

Everywhere he looked, furniture was

stacked high. There were upholstered chairs, daybeds and sofas, but all these had been gnawed by the rats and mice. They would have to be fully restored in order to be used, but the beautifully carved woodwork was still intact.

Penny pointed at these damaged items. 'There is a local family who are experts in upholstery. I shall make sure I purchase sufficient material to have these restored to their former glory. I don't believe you will need to buy anything else to furnish your house. By the by, are the bedchambers furnished?'

'The mattresses will need replacing, and the hangings; but like these, the woodwork is sound. As we are here, do you wish to look in the other rooms, or have you seen enough?'

'We have spent more than enough time up here, Edward. I still have to examine the other reception rooms. Did you get your foreman to measure the windows and walls for me?'

'He is doing that now and should have the list ready when we get down. It seems a shame not to at least look in the other rooms, as this one has proved so successful.'

Reluctantly she agreed, and he stepped around her and pushed open the door in the centre of the wall. Again they cleaned the windows so they could see without the candles. This room was full of bookcases, smaller items of furniture and dozens of boxes of cutlery, silverware, glassware and ornaments. It seemed strange to her that the family heirlooms had been left up here and not taken wherever the previous owner had gone.

There was one more room to investigate on this side of the house. There were three similar attics on the other, but they had to be accessed through a different staircase.

The final attic had trunks stacked from end to end. 'Good heavens! There must be over a hundred in here. We cannot possibly open them all. Which ones shall we look in before we leave?'

Edward strolled across and unstrapped

the first trunk he came to, pushed back the bolts and flung open the lid. He did the same for another half dozen. Inside were bolts of material of every colour one could possibly imagine. There were silks, satins, chiffons, brocades and muslins.

'There is enough here to set up as a modiste in the most expensive part of town,' Penny finally said when she had recovered her voice. 'Where did it all come from? Why should this relative of yours have enough materials to clothe a hundred women?'

'I've no idea, sweetheart, but I shall make enquiries from my lawyers. I know little about this person but intend to find out as much as I can. Because it has been safely sealed away, there is no rodent damage, and the colours have remained as bright as when the materials were made. I'll have the trunks taken to the Lodge, and you and your sisters can have as many gowns as you desire.'

Her cheeks coloured and she remembered her silly remark about him replacing her wardrobe. 'I was not serious about expecting you to foot the bill for fresh gowns for us all. We have more than enough that we brought with us when we came. They have been languishing in the back of our closets, as they are too fine to wear — or rather they were too fine. Now they will be perfect for our new status.'

'Nevertheless, I shall have them transported so you can examine them in more salubrious surroundings. Why don't you return home whilst I examine the rest of these trunks? I'm eager to know what else might be up here that is of value.'

'Then I shall leave you to your discoveries, Edward, and go and find the foreman and collect the list he has made for me.'

She paused on the nursery floor to shake off the worst of the cobwebs and dust, but was acutely conscious of the large section of her petticoat she had torn off. At least when she was wearing a riding habit, the state of her undergarment could not possibly be noticeable.

Certainly, she was treated no differently than she had been on her arrival. The foreman handed her a much blotted and scratched-out list that was barely legible. She carefully folded it and tucked it into the pocket in her skirt.

'Exactly when will the house be ready for occupation?'

'All the major works have been completed, Miss Bradshaw. It's just the hangings, wallpaper and such that need doing. I reckon it could be ready in a month. The master has had a new kitchen put in — you'll get your meals piping hot in future. Would you like to see — '

'It is no concern of mine. Thank you for this. You and your men have done an excellent job.'

As she cantered down the drive, she smiled wryly. If the renovations to the kitchens were no concern of hers, then why had she thanked him for his work as if she was to be mistress of the place?

Edward slammed shut the trunks as soon as she had gone. He had absolutely no interest in their contents but had just wished her to go. The more he saw of her, the stronger his desire. He kicked the wall and immediately regretted it. His dearest Jemima had not driven him wild with passion, and he had been able to spend time with her without behaving badly.

The sooner he found Penelope Bradshaw a husband, the better it would be for both of them. He could never ask her to be his wife, as she would know any vows exchanged would be meaningless in law. She would know that any children they had would be bastards.

He pulled the trunks with material into the centre of the space so they would be easily recognisable when he sent servants up to collect them. In future he must stay away from her, make every effort not to be alone, and certainly never invite her to accompany him as he had today.

When the lawyers came, he would ask them if it would be possible for him to become the guardian of the younger girls — although this too could not have any legal weight because it would be set up in his false identity.

Despite these problems, he was more invigorated than he had been in years. Not since he had spent three years away from his ancestral home at Oxford had he felt as happy and as free. If it wasn't for the inconvenience of finding Penny so damned attractive, life would be all but perfect.

He stopped to admire what had been done and was impressed by the standard of the work. He explained his requirements as to paint and asked his foreman not only to remove the trunks and have them carted to the Lodge, but also to have all the furniture brought down. 'I understand there is a family expert in repair and upholstery. Have them come here to work. The mattresses also need replacing. Is there someone in the village who keeps geese and will be able to restuff them?'

'Leave it to me, master. I'll get things in hand.'

His gelding, this one called Sydney, a remarkably dull name for an excellent beast, was waiting and eager to go. He took a circuitous route back, which allowed Sydney to stretch his legs in a couple of excellent gallops.

On his return, the first thing he noticed as he trotted towards his destination was a smart travelling carriage turning into the drive. He was surprised, but pleased, that the response to his notes had been so prompt. The occupants of this vehicle must be either his banker or his lawyers.

He arrived at the same time as the carriage rocked to a halt outside the front door. He had barely time to dismount before the two boys and the groom appeared to take charge of the horses. The footman arrived to let down the steps and open the door.

'Good afternoon, gentlemen. You

have responded to my request with alacrity. Come in; I have much to ask you to do.'

His lawyer and his clerk scurried alongside him as he led them to the library, half-expecting to find it occupied by the young lady he was hoping to avoid in future. But the chamber was empty.

He gestured the two gentlemen to take the seats on one side of the desk, and he took the single chair on the other side. He explained his requirements in detail and waited for the response. The clerk was still scribbling busily, making sure every word was recorded.

'If Lady Bradshaw is in agreement, sir, then there's no reason why you should not assume legal responsibility for the family. However, I must point out that if the holder of the title and the estate objects, then I will not be able to proceed.'

'That won't happen. He evicted Lady Bradshaw from her home before he arrived.'

'Monstrous. Therefore, I need only to speak to Lady Bradshaw and I can set things in motion.'

As Edward had yet to speak to the lady himself, he thought this might be better postponed until later. 'And the new tenancy agreement? Will there be any difficulty with that?'

'None at all. I can have that ready for you and delivered to Mr Turner tomorrow or the next day.' The lawyer cleared his throat. 'Forgive me for suggesting this, Mr Trevelyan, but I think it might be advisable if you did not become personally involved in the eviction. I have the name of an excellent gentleman who is looking for the position of estate manager. He is the youngest son of Lord Thorogood and wishes to make his own way in the world. I can have him here for you to meet him by the end of the week.'

'That won't be necessary. I trust your judgement. The position is his if he wants it. His first task will be to assemble a group of men and remove those villains from my properties.'

'Mr Thorogood wished to become a soldier, but now that peace has been restored, there is little call for fresh blood in the army. I have met him myself and I'm sure he will be satisfactory in every respect.'

'Tell me a little more about him. How old is he? How would you describe him?'

'He is three-and-twenty, about your height and build but with dark hair and dark eyes. A handsome young man and well-spoken, as one might expect from his upbringing, and a gentleman.'

'How does he have the qualifications to run an estate of this size?'

'He spent his formative years with his father's estate manager. He has also worked with Capability Brown, and I'm sure he could redesign your park if you so wished.'

'I'm happy with it as it is. As long as he can run the estate efficiently, collect the tithes and rents, then I'll be satisfied.'

Coffee and freshly baked pastries were fetched in and devoured eagerly. Whilst they were enjoying the refreshments, he went in search of Lady Bradshaw.

'My lady, I have a suggestion to make that will benefit you all. If I was to become guardian of your daughters, then I can settle a dowry on each without there being any adverse comment. I believe it will make our situation much easier when we are living at the Hall.'

'I am happy to agree to that, Mr Trevelyan. You are the kindest and most generous of gentlemen, and I thank the good Lord that you wandered into our lives.'

The lawyer spoke briefly to her and was satisfied that he had her agreement. The legal team left, promising to have things arranged in a matter of days.

Edward was pleased with the outcome of this meeting, and even more pleased when a gig arrived with his banker and the necessary funds for Penny to purchase what was needed in London. This Tristan Thorogood sounded the ideal husband for Penny. He was going to do everything in his power to promote a match between them, including offering them the Lodge as their future home. The young man might not have an inheritance to look forward to, but he was from an excellent family equal in status to hers, and with the generous settlement he intended to give her they would do very well together.

If he had been free to do so, he would have married her himself, and the thought of her belonging to another was tearing him apart. He did not love her, not in the way he had loved Jemima, but he was forced to admit he had never felt this way about another woman. Penny filled his thoughts, and these were not romantic dreams but passionate and quite unsuitable in the circumstances.

He really should find himself a mistress and slake his desires with her, but for some reason the only woman he wanted to make love to was the woman he could not have.

8

With the arrival of the trunks, full of exciting treasures, Penny's sisters and mother were fully occupied and had little interest in her plans to travel to London the following week. This suited Penny very well as, if Mama stopped to consider, she would realise how unsuitable the journey was for someone like her to attempt.

Edward had appeared only for dinner and then remained just to play a few hands of his strange but enjoyable whist. This was probably for the best after they had both behaved so disgracefully in the attic.

Penny kept herself busy, went riding most days, and tried to convince herself that she didn't care if she spent no time with Edward. The morning of her departure arrived and the carriage was waiting outside to convey Mary her maid, and the footman, to the hostelry where the stagecoach pulled in to collect passengers and change the team.

Sam was dressed in a smart tweed jacket and looked every inch an indoor servant. Penny had already reserved three seats on the coach and requested that they be on the same side so she did not have to sit with strangers.

The other occupants of the coach were unremarkable; she took no notice of them and they did the same to her. They stopped in Colchester at the Red Lion, where they had half an hour to use the facilities and get refreshments before rejoining the vehicle and continuing to London.

Eventually they trundled into the final stop in the late afternoon. Penny was heartily sick of being jostled and jolted, and was more than ready to disembark.

'I have appointments at three warehouses tomorrow. We are going to stay the night in a hotel near Bond Street and then I have booked a carriage to convey us there. When I have completed my purchases, we shall return to the hotel. You will then have the remainder of the day and evening to explore the city. We shall be leaving the following morning on the six o'clock stage. Is that quite clear?'

Sam nodded and Mary curtsied. They were overjoyed to be there, never having visited the capital before. She proposed to give them a shilling or two to spend on whatever they chose. Her intention was to get a hackney carriage to Hanover Square whilst they were elsewhere and try and speak to a servant working in the Bentley town house.

The landlord at the inn arranged for a gig to take them to the hotel, and she was satisfied with her choice. The place was respectable, clean and well-run, but not prestigious, so she was unlikely to meet anyone from her previous life. She had had one Season, and had received three excellent offers, but none of the gentlemen had appealed to her so she had returned unmarried. Mama had been disappointed, but her father had been delighted he wasn't going to lose his favourite child so soon.

She blinked back tears at the thought of him and her dearest brother. They had not even held a funeral as there had been no bodies to bury. She didn't think she would ever quite get over the loss of the two people she loved most in this world.

After a palatable dinner, Penny retired early. Her servants had box rooms close by her. Her excursion to the warehouses was tiring but successful. The proprietors of these places had at first been reluctant to deal with her, as women had no authority to deal with such matters in their opinion. However, when she waved the bank drafts under their noses, they were only too happy to serve her. The materials and so on she had ordered were to be delivered the following week. She had paid an exorbitant extra sum for this to happen, so she hoped they would keep to their part of the bargain.

Sam and Mary were festooned with brown paper parcels and boxes when they returned to the hotel that afternoon. 'Put them in my chamber; they will be safer there. I am quite exhausted and intend to rest and then dine early.' Penny held out a handful of coins. 'Take these; there should be enough there for you to attend a theatre performance if you so desire, and also buy yourself a meal this evening. Do not stay out after dark — and Mary, make sure you are ready to attend to me at five tomorrow.'

They left, laughing and excited, and Penny was glad she had been able to help them have an enjoyable time. The fact that she only did it so she could attend to her other business, and do so privately, did not make the gesture any less valuable in her opinion.

The bonnet she had chosen hid her face in its wide brim, and her gown was well cut but unremarkable. She was certain she could move through the crowds and not be noticed. She had deliberately chosen a hotel near Bond Street, as this was within walking distance of Hanover Square.

She wasn't sure how she was going to achieve her objective, but was certain something would occur to her when she reached her destination. Fortune favoured her, as a woman emerged from the servants' exit as she arrived.

'Excuse me, could you tell me if this is the residence of Lord Bentley?'

The woman nodded. 'It is, miss, but there is no one here.'

'I had thought they were up for the Season.'

'They were, though I can't think why, seeing as the young master was so sickly. It was a real tragedy him dying in a duel, but he would have been dead within a week or two anyway.'

Penny was stunned by this answer. 'Did he suffer from the ague?'

'No, bless you, he had a tumour. It fair broke our hearts to see him suffer so. I think he set out deliberately to get

149

himself killed as he couldn't bear the pain no more.'

'What a sad story. Thank you for your assistance.' Penny quickly walked away before she could be asked why she had come to the house in the first place.

This was the most exciting news, and she could not wait to share it with Edward. It threw a quite different complexion on the event that had caused him to abandon his previous life so suddenly. She returned to the hotel and ordered an early dinner to be served in her room.

The more she thought about this extraordinary information, the less certain she was that it would make any difference to Edward's situation. The housekeeper, if that was who she was, might well have been speaking the truth. Lord Bentley had deliberately provoked Edward into challenging him and then somehow thrown himself into the path of the bullet so that he would be killed and his suffering ended.

It was indeed a tragedy — not just for

the young man who had died, but also for Edward, who had lost his life as well. He had not died, but Lord Stonham could never exist again in public, so in some respects he might as well have done.

*   *   *

Thorogood turned out to be as suitable as Edward been told; articulate, attractive and efficient. He was joining the household until they moved and would then have the Lodge to himself. It was rather a grand house for an estate manager, though this young man wasn't a usual factor, but an aristocrat like himself. Edward had wondered if the young man would expect to be treated with more deference than his other employees, but that wasn't the case.

'I cannot thank you enough for taking me on unseen, Mr Trevelyan. This is exactly the opportunity I was looking for, and I can promise you that you won't be disappointed. I also don't expect to be treated like a member of the household. I will eat in the kitchen with your other staff.'

'You'll do no such thing, Thorogood. You have as much right to be here as I do.'

'Excuse me for disagreeing with you, Mr Trevelyan. I can assure you that her ladyship would be horrified to find me at her table. You are not familiar with the ways of aristocrats, but I am, unfortunately.'

'Then I shall be guided by you. Now, let us discuss how you intend to remove those objectionable men from my properties.'

'I think that cudgels and fisticuffs will not be sufficient. From what I've learned in the short time I've been here, they are armed to the teeth. They have several ex-soldiers in their employ who will no doubt be equipped with rifles or at least muskets.'

'God's teeth! I won't have those who go on my behalf hurt. Do you have a suggestion as to how this can be achieved without bloodshed?'

'I think I do. They are living there illegally because they have failed to pay their rent the past seven years. Therefore, I have taken the liberty of writing to the magistrate and asking if he can send constables, or even the militia, to remove them for us.'

'I'm impressed; I should have thought of that myself. So they must remain where they are for the present. I see that you came with your own horse. Do you have a valet to take care of your needs?'

Thorogood smiled at the question. 'I'm used to taking care of my own requirements, sir. I have no need of a manservant.' He patted the pile of books and documents. 'I should take these to the small room I have found on the other side of the house. It will be ideal for me to use as my office.'

Edward had been about to tell him he could remain in the library but thought better of it. When he had been heir to an earldom, he would not have tolerated the presence of even the estate manager at the table in his library.

He strolled to the window and stared out thoughtfully. His offer for Thorogood to become part of the household had been genuine, not part of his deception. It was ironic that his behaviour was exactly right for the person he was supposed to be. How could he have changed so much in so short a time?

He was now a gentleman of leisure again with no responsibilities. His new employee had taken over the running of his estates and was probably more competent than he was himself to do so. The house seemed empty without Penny, and he was looking forward to her return the next day.

He was waylaid by Lady Bradshaw as he was about to leave the house. 'There you are, my dear boy. You have been proving very elusive these past few days. I cannot thank you enough for the boxes of delights that you have presented us with. My dressmaker and her seamstresses will be working overtime sewing all of us fresh gowns.'

'There are twice as many trunks unopened in the attics of the Hall, my lady. When we have moved, you must go up and investigate and see if there is anything else there that you might like.'

'How exciting! Have you any notion how this distant relative of yours might have acquired these items? Was he perhaps about to set up an emporium dealing with expensive materials?'

'I know little about him. In fact if I'm honest, nothing at all. I am still uncertain how they discovered my existence, as I think I must be as distantly related to him as the unpleasant character who has now usurped your family home.'

'There was enough in just one trunk to make two dozen gowns, far more than we shall ever need this year. Mrs Reynolds, my dressmaker, has intimated that if you were to open an establishment of this sort, she would be only too delighted to run it for you.' She waved her hands around and was more animated than he'd ever seen her. 'I have the connections that would bring the high-end trade to such a place.'

He was astonished that her ladyship should be so enthusiastic about anything that smacked of trade. 'I'm intrigued by your suggestion, my lady, and will give it consideration. Perhaps Miss Bradshaw would like to be involved? Forgive me for asking, but are you quite sure you wish to be associated with something of this ilk?'

'Fiddlesticks to that! My dear departed husband inherited a moderate fortune and then by his acumen doubled it. He was so astute I cannot believe he did not keep the money made from his import and export business separate from what was entailed.'

'Did he travel abroad often?'

'He was away for several months most years. Why do you ask?'

'In which case, my lady, I'm certain he did make those arrangements. He must have known there was always a risk that he and your son could lose their lives. Travelling abroad is not a safe occupation.'

'If that was so, then why did the family lawyers not pass this money on to me?'

'I have no idea, but I intend to find out.'

She was effusive in her thanks, which made him even more determined to discover why the family had been left virtually penniless when there must be a small fortune somewhere that belonged to them. He had not taken more than a few steps from the house when Thorogood appeared from the side entrance. Edward beckoned him over.

'There is something I need you to do for me.' He explained and the young man frowned.

'There is something illegitimate involved here, sir, it should definitely be investigated. I am just about to ride to Ipswich to set in motion the eviction of your tenants and can combine the two tasks. Do I have your permission to remain overnight?'

'Good God, you do not have to ask me that. You are free to come and go as your work takes you without seeking my agreement. All I ask is that you let me know if you are going to be elsewhere.'

'That is good to know. I shall do my job far better knowing that you trust me to work independently.'

'I am going to visit the Hall. I think it would be useful for you to come with me.'

They rode the short distance in companionable silence. He was glad this young man did not feel the need to fill every moment with idle chatter.

He was pleased how much had been done in the past day. The stairs and hall were finished. The pieces of furniture he had selected from the mountain upstairs had been placed perfectly and only needed ornaments or flowers to complete the picture.

'The things that need repair and restoration, Mr Trevelyan, have been taken to one of the barns. They will be stripped back and ready for upholster-ing by the time the fabric arrives from London. New mattresses are being made, and they too will be delivered by the end of next week or soon after. The two bathing rooms you have had installed are ready for inspection. Would you like to see how they work?'

Seeing the water that had been tipped into the tub vanish like magic down a small aperture at the far end was quite astonishing. Even young Thorogood was impressed.

'I've heard about such things but never seen it myself. It will make the task of the chambermaids so much easier if they only have to transport water up and not carry the dirty down.'

The foreman scratched his head. 'Can't see the point meself. You'll not be using it more than a handful of times a year. Hardly worth the effort, I reckon.'

Edward couldn't help himself stiffen at this inappropriate comment from a servant and only just managed to restrain himself from giving the man a sharp set-down. 'Is the new range now working?'

'It is, sir, and mighty fine too.'

Hopefully neither of the men had noticed his displeasure, as he had covered it by his question. He cared nothing about the workings of his kitchen, but his question had distracted both of them.

'I should dearly like to see it before I depart,' Thorogood said eagerly.

'I'm going to have another look in the attic, so I'll leave you to it.'

Now that the windows in the attics were relatively clean there was no need for him to seek out a candle. The first chamber was empty of furniture, as it had all been removed. There would be a large bonus for all the men involved in this enterprise, as they had worked efficiently and quickly at all the tasks they had been set.

The second attic was also half-empty, as the trunks he and Penny had examined were already at the Lodge. It would do no harm to see what else was up here, as he was half inclined to take up Lady Bradshaw's suggestion and open an emporium in Ipswich selling the most expensive materials to discerning clients. He had not been over-interested in women's fashion, but even he recognised that what he had discovered so far was of the best quality and would be much in demand.

The other trunks were filled with a kaleidoscope of coloured items, silk threads, ribbons, exotic feathers and a plethora of items that would be snatched up with alacrity by any lady that saw them. The third room revealed even greater treasures. In these boxes were dozens of silver items, sandalwood boxes, and carvings.

He pulled them into the space in the centre of the room where he could move about without cracking his head on the beams, and looked around for something to smash open the locks. After searching through several trunks, he came across a scimitar with strange writing engraved on the blade and jewels embedded in the hilt.

This weapon was used to fight, so

should be strong enough for his purpose. He slid the blade between the padlock and the chest and threw his weight against it, half-expecting it to break. Instead, the padlock flew free and the blade remained intact. He carefully pushed it back into its scabbard. He thought that this and all the other items must have come from India — it certainly had the appearance of being from that far-off place.

9

Penny was bubbling with excitement, and even the hours in the uncomfortable coach did nothing to dampen her enthusiasm. She wished that the information she had discovered would allow Edward to resume his proper persona, but at least she now would not feel guilty about the death of the unfortunate man who had already been dying.

There was one thing that puzzled her. Why hadn't Bentley taken his own life? She understood that committing suicide would bring disgrace to his family name, but surely he could have arranged to drown himself, fall off his horse and break his neck, and end his life and suffering without involving Edward?

She came to the conclusion that using a Stonham as his executioner had been because of the long-standing feud between the families. It must have seemed like the perfect opportunity to destroy the happiness of those that they considered their enemies.

She was squashed against the window and she could barely see her maid or footman beneath the parcels they had stacked on their laps. She could have had these things sent with the order, but preferred to bring them back with her so she could give her family some well-deserved gifts. The fact that Edward had paid for them made no difference as far as she was concerned. As she had taken the trouble to travel to London and then buy the items, she was their benefactor and not him.

The coach was waiting to collect them, and in no time at all they were all reinstalled and on their way back to the Lodge. 'I hope you enjoyed your short visit to town?' Penny said to her companions. 'I could not have accomplished what I did without your assistance, and I thank you for it.'

Thanking one's servants would be

frowned upon, especially by Edward, but she had never held with convention and had always behaved as she thought appropriate. Papa had encouraged her to behave more like her brother, and not having either of them there to support her would always be painful.

There was no time for further morbid thoughts as the carriage turned into the drive and she was home. She hoped dinner had been postponed as she was sharp-set, having not eaten since breakfast, which was many hours ago.

Her sisters ran from the house, squealing with delight like children. Laughing, Penny jumped out, not waiting for the steps to be let down, and embraced them both. 'I am so glad to be back. I have gifts for you all, but they must wait until after I have eaten.'

'Mama has been complaining she is faint with hunger this past hour, and dear Edward is doing his best to distract her,' Mattie said.

Penny was shocked that her sister was now addressing him so familiarly.

Surely they should call him at least Cousin Edward?

'What have you bought for us? Can you tell us even if we cannot look?' Beth asked.

'I shall reveal nothing. I had intended to change, but if our parent is so desperate to dine I had better restrict myself to a quick wash.'

'You must take all the time you need, my dear. You have been travelling for hours and need to refresh yourself.' Edward had met them in the hall.

'I thank you, but I shall be as speedy as I can. Could you have my parcels left in the drawing room?'

She didn't wait to see if he complied; she knew he would. What she would really like to do was take him to one side and tell him what she had learned, but this too must wait until after dinner.

A fresh muslin gown in daffodil yellow was waiting for her. With the help of her sisters' maid, she was clean and freshly garbed in less than a quarter of an hour.

Her mother greeted her with a frown. 'At last, Penelope. You have kept us waiting quite long enough for our dinner.'

'I was as quick as I could be, Mama. Shall we go in?'

Her mother stalked across the room like a ship in full sail, and her sisters were not far behind. Edward offered his arm and she took it.

'Surprisingly, sweetheart, I have missed you and am inordinately pleased to see you home again.'

'I am delighted to be back. I have much to tell you. Would you walk in the garden with me after dinner?'

'I should be delighted.'

His smile made her toes curl in her slippers.

The meal was excellent, but nobody wished to linger over it, so conversation was sparse. Mama and the girls, knowing there were exciting items to unwrap in the drawing room, ate in silence. Penny and Edward were equally eager to finish and be able to converse in private.

Her mother all but threw her napkin

down and surged to her feet. 'Come along; I am done. I must know what you have brought us back from London. It is too long since we had treats of any sort.'

Edward got to his feet too, not lingering over port, and so they all made their way into the drawing room. Penny would have to distribute the items herself, as they were not labelled, and she knew which parcel was meant for which person.

'Don't open anything until I have handed all the items out.'

Even Edward had four things to unwrap. He raised an eyebrow and she smiled sweetly. He was well aware that he was his own benefactor.

He put his gifts on a side table and walked towards the open doors at the far end of the drawing room that led onto the terrace. Penny's family was so busy exclaiming and shrieking with delight that they didn't notice she too had left them.

'I take it you have no coins to return to me,' he said dryly.

'Actually, I have. Obviously I do not have the money about my person, but I shall return it to you when I go in again.'

'I don't give a fig if you spent every penny, sweetheart, but I wish you might have bought something extravagant for yourself and not spent it all on the others.'

'Fiddlesticks to that! I have something to tell you.' She was so carried away with the importance of her tale that she had almost completed it before she became aware he was staring at her not with approval but something akin to fury. Her voice trailed away.

He seemed to be having difficulty speaking. 'What you did was dangerous in the extreme. If I had known you were planning something so stupid, I would never have allowed you to go.'

She gaped at him, unable to comprehend why he was so angry when she had given him news that relieved him of the burden of having killed someone by accident. 'I thought you would be pleased to know Bentley committed suicide at your hand.'

'I don't give a damn what that bastard did. If his father had been there, I shudder to think what might have happened to you.'

She scarcely heard his tirade, so shocked was she by his appalling language.

'Not only that,' he continued, 'but did it not occur to you that making enquiries of this sort would immediately alert the Bentley family to the fact that I am not in fact on the continent but still in England? Was it your intention to have me arrested and dangle at the gallows?'

This last remark was so outrageous she recovered her width and was able to respond. 'Mr Trevelyan, never have I heard such appalling words. You should be ashamed of yourself. If you continue to shout at me, I shall be forced to . . . to . . . ' She could not think of anything she might do that was sufficiently powerful to show her extreme displeasure. Instead she attempted to shove past him, but was overenthusiastic and watched with horror as he vanished backwards over the balustrade.

She did not remain to enquire how he did. His vile swearing indicated he was unhurt in anything but his pride. Now was the time to make a strategic retreat, and the further away the better. She fled inside and raced to her own bedchamber. This was the one place he could not follow. No gentleman visited an unmarried lady in her boudoir.

Mary was busy in the dressing room and rushed in to see what the commotion was. 'Have you eaten?'

'No, miss. I thought it best if I did this before I went down.'

'Leave it; you can complete your task tomorrow morning. I shall not require you anymore this evening.'

The girl curtsied and rushed off, leaving Penny to pace the room trying to make sense of what had just happened. Why had Edward been so angry with her? Speaking to the housekeeper without identifying herself could not possibly cause him any concern. She was recovering her composure when the door

171

opened and he strode in.

'We have not finished our conversation, so do not think you can hide in here.'

'You must leave at once, sir. I am outraged that you have the temerity to enter my bedchamber.'

'That is easily solved. Come into the hall and sit with me on the seat under the oriel window, for I have matters of import to discuss.'

Penny hesitated, but then her curiosity got the better of her and she followed him, both of them sitting down to face one another.

'I beg your pardon for my barrack-room language,' Edward said. 'You would try the patience of a saint, and I have no pretence of being one of those.'

This was hardly a gracious apology, but she thought it was the only one she was going to get. Then she noticed he had greenery attached to his person and a large muddy streak across his cheek. She stood up and removed the bits of plant and then rubbed the mud away with her fingers. It had been an instinctive move, and he remained immobile whilst she did it.

'Have you finished?' he enquired softly.

Her heart skittered and her pulse raced. 'I apologise for pushing you over the balcony, though you must understand it was an accident.'

'Your apology is accepted.' His breath brushed her cheek, and she thought her knees would give way beneath her. She didn't dare look at him for fear of what she would see.

Then his hand cupped her face and gently turned it in his direction. 'I find myself torn in two directions whenever I'm with you, sweetheart. I either wish to make love to you or put you in your place. Which would you prefer?' His eyes were twinkling, so she assumed this was a rhetorical question.

'If I'm to be given a choice, sir, then neither. I must sit down, for I am feeling a little odd.'

Immediately his expression changed to one of concern. 'That is hardly surprising, my love . . . '

She collapsed on the seat before answering. 'Please desist from addressing me so familiarly. I am not your sweetheart, your love or anything else of that ilk.'

He folded his long length on the far end of the seat and swivelled so he could face her. 'Actually, sweetheart, you have mistaken the matter. I am now your legal guardian until you are five-and-twenty, and I am addressing you as I would a younger sibling or daughter.'

So astonished was she by his remark that she laughed out loud. 'You are quite ridiculous, Mr Trevelyan. I suppose this is my mother's idea? It makes sense to me that you have become my sisters' protector, but I am in no need of anyone's guidance or protection.'

'Now we have got that out of the way, I must speak to you about what you told me. I can state categorically that Bentley did not throw himself in front of my bullet — he remained exactly where he was. I am certain he deliberately set out to have me arraigned for his murder.'

* * *

As he spoke, Edward was running through the scenario of the duel in his head. There was only one possible explanation for what had taken place, and it was so extraordinary he could not credit that it was what had taken place.

'I think the whole thing was contrived to make me look guilty. The three men with him must have been part of the plot.'

'Contrived?' She frowned and bit her lip for a moment, then her eyes widened. 'I believe that I know how it was done. I once saw a mummers' play in which someone was murdered. The villain appeared to stab the victim, and immediately his shirt front was stained red. I was only a child, and I was suitably horrified until my father reassured me it was a trick.'

'Pig's blood hidden behind his shirt

and then released at the exact moment my bullet would have struck him. The so-called surgeon and his two seconds had him back in the carriage before I could investigate, even if I had wished to do so. I was too shocked to think straight at that point.'

'I expect you were more concerned about leaving the scene before you could be arrested.'

'The constables were about to arrive. Now I come to consider this matter, it was strange indeed they were so close. Someone alerted them and it certainly wasn't me.'

'This is even better than I thought. If Lord Bentley died from natural causes, then your name will be cleared and you can assume your life as an aristocrat.'

The thought of returning to the restricted existence he had had did not appeal to him. 'I think it will be impossible to prove, Penny, but at least my conscience is clear. You took a dreadful risk on my behalf, but I should have been grateful and not shouted at you the way I did.'

She peeped at him from behind her lashes, and an all too familiar surge of heat went through him.

'I think we are even on that score, Edward, as you had your comeuppance when you fell in the flower bed.'

'It will be the talk of the village soon enough, as there were two groundsmen working in the shrubbery when I landed in the dirt.'

'Oh dear! Do you think they saw me shove you?'

'I'm certain they did not. Remember the terrace is at a higher level, so anything that takes place there is not visible to those below.'

'My reputation is somewhat tarnished after gallivanting to London on my own, so I'm relieved it will not be further stained by appearing to be a violent young lady.'

He didn't tell her that from this moment forward, she and her sisters would be not only be from an aristocratic family but also wealthy heiresses.

Of course, they could have their pick of the gentlemen available if they attended a London Season, but that wasn't possible in the circumstances.

He was sure there would be no shortage of eager suitors once word of their availability became known. Mattie and Beth were probably too young to marry — in fact they were more like schoolroom girls than young women ready to embark on matrimony.

Belatedly it occurred to Edward that investigating too deeply into this distant relative might reveal his own identity, but it was too late to repine. He was certain Thorogood would not betray him even if he did discover his secret.

'We had better return to the drawing room before my mother comes to erroneous conclusions from our absence. Have you told her about the treasure?'

'Good God! I should think not. I am very fond of your mama, but I do not believe she is the soul of discretion any more than your sisters are. I know I can trust you to keep any secrets to yourself.'

He offered his hand, but she ignored it and rose gracefully to her feet without assistance. She was a remarkable young lady, and the better he knew her the more he liked her. He feared he was already headlong in love with her. What he had believed to be love between Jemima and himself had been nothing in comparison to the strength of his feelings now.

If he remained under the same roof as Penny, it was inevitable he would compromise her. Had he not kissed her? Only a betrothed couple could exchange kisses, and that was something they could never be in his present circumstances.

He wished with all his heart that she had not discovered he was a dissembler, because as she had pointed out to him, if his future bride did not know the true circumstances, she would never be aware she was not legally his wife.

Papa had said blithely that one day his grandson would inherit the title, but that was not the case. Any sons he might have would be considered illegitimate and not eligible to become the Earl of Stonham. This was an insoluble problem, and he would not embroil her further in his sordid affairs. From now on, he would keep a distance between them and do everything he could to promote a union between her and Thorogood.

10

Penny could not help but be aware Edward was avoiding her. She had no idea why this was so, and she missed not being able to spar with him. Now they had a full complement of staff, she had little to do to occupy her time.

Her sisters and mother were happy to devour the latest fashion plates and plan their new wardrobe, but this did not interest her. As far as she was concerned, she had more than enough gowns, even if they were not the latest style.

The addition to the household of Mr Thorogood was something she approved of. He was a young man of impeccable manners and ready wit, and was a fine figure of a man. When he invited her to ride with him, she accepted without hesitation.

'My sisters are too busy selecting

material for their new wardrobe to resent me monopolising the mare. Mr Trevelyan intends to buy more rides for us but is somewhat preoccupied with this business at his farms for the present.'

'I have not ridden to all the hamlets, cottages and farms that are in this demesne. I shall not attempt to speak to either of the tenants that are about to be evicted, but I would like to see for myself what needs doing on this estate so I can set things in motion for my employer.'

'That sounds a splendid morning's excursion. It will only take me a moment to change into my habit — perhaps you would be good enough to ask one of the stable boys to tack up for me?'

When she returned, her mount was ready and she gathered the reins, put one hand on the pommel and turned so he could toss her into the saddle. He did this with consummate ease. She was rather enjoying having two handsome gentlemen in her life, even if one of them was avoiding her at the moment.

After an enjoyable few hours, she returned well satisfied with her companion. Edward had done well to employ such an excellent gentleman. His family were as well placed in society as hers had been, but perhaps not as elevated as Edward's.

She dropped to the ground without waiting for his assistance. 'Mr Thorogood, whatever your reservations, I insist that in future you dine with us. I know that you consider yourself an employee, but your pedigree trumps that in my opinion.'

His smile was charming but it didn't make her toes curl. 'Then I should be delighted to join you. Do you dress for dinner?'

'We do not. However, my mother would not be pleased if anyone appeared smelling of the stable.'

His laugh attracted the attention of Edward, who had just ridden into the yard. Penny thought he might be annoyed that she had become friendly with Mr Thorogood, but the reverse was true. He dismounted, tossed his reins to a waiting boy, and strolled across to join them.

'Did you have a pleasant ride? I'm surprised our paths did not cross.'

'Most enjoyable, thank you, Edward. I have persuaded Mr Thorogood to join us for dinner in future.'

She waited to see what his reaction to this announcement might be, but again he smiled benignly. 'I had already asked him the same question but he refused me. I'm glad that you have been success-ful. I should enjoy having someone to drink port with in the evenings.'

She left them to discuss business matters and returned to her bedcham-ber. When she was freshly washed and in one of her prettiest muslins, she hurried downstairs and was disap-pointed to find both gentlemen had gone out again.

The next two days were spent in similar fashion. Penny rode with Mr

Thorogood in the morning and he dined with them in the evening. Her sisters behaved impeccably when he was present, and she noticed that Mattie hung on his every word. She was glad that he treated her like a younger sibling and at no time showed the slightest interest in her as a woman.

Three days after coming back from London, Penny was called to the front of the house by an overexcited Mattie. 'There's a regiment of soldiers trotting up the drive. I've never seen anything so splendid. Why are they here?'

'I think they have come to evict some tenants from Edward's properties. No doubt he and Mr Thorogood will explain it to us tonight over dinner.'

Her sister pouted. 'He doesn't seem as jolly as he was before, especially with you. Have you and he had a falling-out?'

'Not really, but now he is our legal guardian things have changed. I am sure it is better for him to be occupied with his own business and leave us to get on with ours.'

Her sister was no longer listening, for she had rushed to the front door and flung it open. This was not the behaviour of a well brought up young lady. Mattie should have waited until the officer in charge knocked on the door and it was opened by the footman.

'Excuse me, ladies, but this is not your concern. Kindly go back to the drawing room at once.' Edward had arrived behind them and did not seem at all pleased to find them gawping out of the door at the militia.

Mattie was about to protest, but Penny gripped her elbow. 'I beg your pardon, Mr Trevelyan. We are going now.'

She half dragged her reluctant companion into the drawing room. 'You can see quite well from here. Have you no decorum? I am ashamed of your behaviour, and Edward is most displeased.'

There was the sound of running feet, and Beth burst in. 'Have you seen the soldiers outside? Why are they here?'

'I've already asked that and Penny doesn't know. We mustn't be seen to be looking, so shall we go up and watch from our bedchamber instead?'

Penny's sisters ran off, laughing and chattering. Sometimes she felt herself to be ten years their senior and not just five. She had never been so giddy, so silly, even when she was as young as they were. The thought of them let loose in a ballroom full of gentlemen did not bear thinking of.

Mattie was certainly old enough to have her come-out, but Penny would try and persuade Mama to postpone it until next year. When they would both hopefully be more sensible. Having Edward and Mr Thorogood spend time with them in the evenings would hopefully teach both girls how to behave in company.

At least that was something Penny could help with. She would write at once to the agency in Ipswich that was to supply the staff for Ravenswood Hall and set about finding them a suitable governess. They had been much better behaved when in the charge of someone other than herself and their mother.

The letter written, she decided to take it down to the village and leave it at the posting inn herself. It was no more than a brisk three quarters of an hour's walk, and the exercise would do her good. Mary could accompany her, so there could be no possible complaint that she was behaving improperly.

The weather was clement, but her gown was of a light cotton material with only two petticoats beneath it, so she would not get overheated even if she walked fast. Her maid carefully tied the ribbons on the matching bonnet, and hooked up her walking boots, and she was ready.

'We shall go out through the rear entrance. I've no intention of becoming entangled with the soldiers who are milling about at the front and by the stables.'

'Yes, miss. I saw them arrive. I do

think they look ever so smart in their red regimentals.'

'I'm sure they do, Mary, but it is no concern of yours or mine.'

The path to the village cut across the fields, and Penny had never paused to consider which farm's right of way it ran through. In the time they had been living at the Lodge, they had all, apart from Mama, traversed this way many times and never seen a soul.

Now she came to think of it, this was rather strange. Surely she should have seen the occasional farmworker, farm beast or women from the village gleaning the fields?

The first part of the journey took them through a wooded area that was part of the land attached to their home, but after they stepped over the stile they would be on the land of one of Edward's tenants. She had no idea whether where they were walking today was part of the farm that was about to be invaded by the militia or if it was part of another property.

The fact that soldiers were about to evict some tenants made no difference to her, but she was sure Edward must be pleased. She would continue her walk as she always did. Why should anything be different today?

* * *

Edward had no intention of riding with the militia. His task was to make sure the officer knew exactly where he was to lead his men and let them get on with it. He was taking a risk being seen as it was. It had already been decided that Thorogood was to accompany them instead.

'We will arrest the individuals and take them to the jailhouse in Ipswich. We already have your complaint lodged, and the magistrate will deal with the matter speedily. You will not be required to attend — your estate manager can represent you.'

'It might be advisable, Mr Trevelyan, to have the ladies remain inside today.'

Thorogood leaned down from the saddle and spoke quietly.

'Thank you; I should have thought of that myself.'

He strode indoors and discovered Lady Bradshaw engrossed in a pile of periodicals, and he was informed that the younger girls were safely upstairs.

'Penelope has gone to the village to post a letter with her maid. She left a while ago.'

'Thank you, my lady. You have been most helpful.' He nodded and retreated, trying not to show his agitation. Thank God he was already dressed to ride. This was entirely his fault — if he hadn't barked at Penny when he'd seen her earlier, she wouldn't have felt the need to distance herself from him.

In less than ten minutes, he was astride Bruno, and the head groom accompanied him on Sydney. He had no idea in which direction the village was if you travelled on foot, so he needed someone to set him on the right path.

He jumped the stile with feet to clear

and kicked his mount into a flat gallop. According to his groom, they should have been able to see Penny and her maid as the path led for a mile or more across the same field. He only slowed his pace as he approached the outlying cottages of the village, as he had no wish to draw attention to himself.

He sent the groom in to enquire if she had been seen at the inn, and he came out shaking his head. Edward had a bad feeling about this. Any day but today he would not have been worried; would just have assumed she had changed her mind and taken a different route, or gone to visit her friend at the rectory.

However, it would have been hard to miss the arrival of the militia; and the men who were about to be evicted would have had word of this some time ago.

He returned the way he had come and drew rein to speak to his groom. 'You will dismount and walk along the path leading your horse and see if there's anything unusual that catches your eye. I'm going to investigate the far side of the field. I'm damn sure I can see Brook Farm just behind those trees.'

Leaving his servant to look for signs that Penny and her maid had been abducted — a foolish notion, but one he could not ignore — he cantered across the field, making sure he was out of sight of the house at all times.

When he reached the far side of the field, he saw there was a gate leading into the trees behind which he had seen the roof of the farm. He dismounted and quickly pulled the reins over Bruno's head and tied them to the gate. 'Stand here, old fellow. I'll not be long.'

Beneath the trees were tangled brambles, with no sign that anyone had been this way. There was little point in him continuing along this route; he was wasting his time. He untethered his horse, swung into the saddle and turned towards his groom.

The hair on the back of his neck

stood up when he saw the man was waving frantically at him and pointing to the ground. He thundered back across the field, sending divots flying in all directions, and Bruno came to a rearing halt beside the other horse. Edward was on the ground in seconds.

'What have you seen? Why were you waving?'

'Look here, master. You can see hoof prints. Two horses at least have been here; but see — they didn't continue along the path, but returned across the field towards the farm.'

Edward dropped to his knees and pushed aside the long grass in the hope of finding some definitive proof that something untoward had taken place. He saw nothing, and was about to stand up when he glanced down at his glove. The palm was covered with a sticky red substance — it could be nothing else but fresh blood.

He held it up so the groom could see. There was no need to say anything else. They both knew what it meant. This time he vaulted into the saddle and Bruno bucked in protest. He wrenched the animal's head towards home and urged him into a gallop for the second time that day.

He had been gone barely a quarter of an hour. He prayed he would be able to catch up with the militia before they arrived at Brook Farm. If they went in with weapons drawn, he feared for the women's lives.

★   ★   ★

Penny was lost in her thoughts when Mary nudged her in the back with the basket she was carrying over her arm. 'Miss, there's horses coming this way, and I don't like the look of the riders, not one bit.'

Penny turned to stare and her heart plummeted to her boots. 'Run, run back to the stile — they will not follow us once we are back on our own land.'

All might have been well if her maid had not slipped and tumbled to the

195

grass. Although it only took moments for her to regain her feet, it was long enough to make the hundred yards an impossible distance.

'Wait; we shall stand our ground. This is still Mr Trevelyan's land, and we have every right to be on this path.'

She pushed her maid behind her and waited for the horses to arrive. Both animals were unkempt, their coats matted, and obviously underfed. The riders were in little better state. The smell that wafted across made her gag.

There was a hedge behind her, and the two obnoxious ruffians forced them to move backwards until they were pressed against it.

'What do we 'ave 'ere, Jed? I reckon as the master would likes to meet these two fine ladies.' The speaker had lank hair so dirty it was impossible to tell the true colour. His clothes were no better, and Penny was certain he was crawling with vermin.

'Kindly remove yourselves,' she said. 'I am the daughter of Lady Bradshaw, and if you waylay me for a moment longer, I shall report you to the constable.' She was pleased her voice showed none of her fear.

'Now then, missie, no need to get uppity. You'll come along of us easy like or 'ard — it makes no nevermind to me.'

'We shall do no such thing. The punishment for kidnapping is death. You can be very sure my guardian, Mr Trevelyan, will have you prosecuted to the fullest extent of the law.' Her impassioned words had the opposite effect to the one she desired. Perhaps mentioning Edward's name had not been a wise choice given the circumstances.

She wasn't going to go quietly; she would fight for her freedom and make things as difficult as she could. She was certain there was a large stone beneath her feet. If she could just bend down and snatch it up, she would have a weapon that could do serious damage to her would-be abductors.

'Mary, start screaming. Make as much noise as you can to distract them,' she whispered out of the side of her mouth. She did as Penny asked, and the noise had the desired effect.

''Ere, you — stop that racket, or it'll be the worse for you,' the man snarled. He tried to grab Mary but she wriggled away.

This gave Penny the opportunity she needed. She pretended to stumble to her knees in fear and managed to prise up a satisfactorily large stone. When she regained her feet, she kept it hidden in the folds of her skirt.

Mary was ominously silent, but Penny didn't dare look to see what was happening to her maid. The second evil-smelling villain leaned down in his saddle, intending to grab her and haul her up in front of him.

Penny struck him as hard as she could on his head. He tumbled to the grass without a sound. Without a second thought, she grabbed the reins of his horse and scrambled into the saddle.

This manoeuvre had taken scarcely a minute. Now she was mounted and was less vulnerable.

'Go, miss, it's you they want,' Mary screamed at her.

Penny had managed to mount without dropping her weapon. She was an expert horsewoman and turned the wretched beast around with ease so she was facing the other attacker.

He was struggling to hold on to Mary, and his mouth dropped open in shock when he realised what had happened to his friend. Two sharp kicks in the horse's side was all it took to bring the animal close to him. She felled him in the same way, and he collapsed to his knees, groaning loudly.

'Give me your hand, Mary. I'll pull you up behind me. We must get away from here before they recover.'

Somehow they managed to achieve this without Penny being pulled from the saddle. Just in time, as the man on his knees was now staggering to his feet, swearing vilely and threatening to murder her when he got his hands around her throat.

She had a split second to come to a decision. They couldn't jump the stile on this nag without coming to grief. There was a similar one at the far end of the field that led to the village. She could hardly go in the direction from which these brigands had come. This meant she must find a way through the hedge and escape that way.

The horse refused to do more than trot, but it was enough to take them temporarily out of danger. Another hundred yards and she saw what she wanted. She wrenched the left-hand rein and kicked the horse as hard as she could.

'Hold on, we're going through this gap.'

The thorns and branches tore her skirts. Her bonnet was long gone. Mary's arms were still gripping fiercely around her waist as the horse shouldered his way through the hedge and into the field beyond.

'Come on, boy. One last effort and I

promise you a life of luxury in future.'

The horse flicked his ears and lurched into a surprisingly comfortable canter. She patted his neck and crooned to him. It did the trick, and he lengthened his stride, taking them both to safety.

On the far side of this field was a track which led out onto a lane she recognised. 'This leads to Ravenswood Hall. We'll be safe there.'

Gently, Penny pulled on the reins and eased the horse to a walk. It wouldn't do to have him collapse before they got there. The track emerged behind the stables, and their sudden appearance caused an unfortunate workman to drop his bucket of whitewash on his feet.

Mary slithered to the ground and she joined her. 'Can you take care of this unfortunate animal? He needs a good feed and a groom. I promised him he would be taken care of.'

The man had recovered from his shock and yelled over his shoulder for assistance. Several men came running, and amongst them was the foreman she had met before. When she explained what had transpired, he was first concerned that they were hurt, and then furious that they should have been attacked in this way.

'You go along into the house, Miss Bradshaw. There's womenfolk will take care of you until Mr Trevelyan can come with the coach and take you home.'

'I thank you; we'll do as you suggest.'

Mary seemed remarkably resilient after her experience. 'Now that it's over, miss, I quite enjoyed it. It's not every day you get abducted.'

'Fortunately, it was only an attempted abduction.'

'Only because you knocked the blighters down, miss. I've never seen the like.'

Penny stopped listening as something more interesting was taking place amongst the labourers, carpenters and other workmen. Led by the foreman, they had gathered their tools and were intending to set off to confront the tenant of Brook Farm.

11

Bruno was not as eager to jump from the field into the darkness of the wood, but did not refuse. Edward kicked the beast into a headlong gallop; not the wisest move when travelling under trees. He flattened himself against the horse's neck and narrowly avoided being unseated more than once.

The path through the wood emerged onto the track that led around the back of the stables and from there joined up with the lane that the militia would be taking. This was an all-mounted brigade, but they were not travelling at speed as he was, and he soon caught up with them.

He steadied Bruno to a collected canter and yelled for the soldiers at the rear to move aside. They did so, and he passed between them safely and arrived at the head of the column.

'Thorogood, Lieutenant, I believe that Miss Bradshaw and her maid have been abducted and possibly taken to Brook Farm.' He quickly explained how he had come to this extraordinary conclusion. 'I beg you to be circumspect when you arrive.'

'We shall take every precaution, Mr Trevelyan. You can leave the safety of your ward to us. I can guarantee she will come to no further harm and will be returned to you.' Thorogood had metamorphosed into a formidable young man; obviously the thought that Penny was in danger was enough to harden his resolve.

Edward nodded and moved his mount to one side to allow them to ride past. He cursed inwardly that he was helpless to go to Penny's aid himself. It should be he who rescued her, not that jackanapes.

The groom was waiting on the verge for him to come back. 'Return to the Lodge. I'm going to the Hall.' He had no wish to be obliged to inform Lady

Bradshaw that her daughter had possibly been kidnapped. He shuddered at the thought of how this lady might react.

He was more than a hundred yards away from his destination when he quite clearly heard Penny's voice. He kicked the gelding into a gallop. His arrival sent the group of men that had gathered around her scattering to avoid being trampled underfoot.

He was off his horse and at her side in seconds. 'Sweetheart, thank God you are safe. I thought you had been taken by those villains from Brook Farm.'

'I am so glad you are here. Please tell these men that they must not march on the farm themselves. I am, as you can see, relatively unscathed by my unpleasant experience. The militia can deal with whoever tried to abduct me far better than these brave men who are not armed with anything other than cudgels and work implements.'

'I thank you for your intentions, men, but Miss Bradshaw is correct. Please return to your work.' The words were polite but his voice was firm. They didn't argue and dispersed immediately.

'Tell me at once what took place. I found blood on the grass and thought it was yours.'

When she had finished her story, he was horrified. 'You could have been murdered if they had got hold of you after your attack. I'm not sure if I am proud of your exploits or not.'

'I have told you before, I am a resourceful lady and well able to take care of myself. I still have a letter to deliver, and if it is to catch the mail coach, it must be taken directly.'

With a sigh of resignation, he held out his hand, and she reached into her habit pocket and handed him the missive. 'Thank you, sir. That is most gracious of you. Mary and I will remain here until you can send the carriage to collect us. As you might have noticed, I am somewhat dishevelled.' She held out her skirt and shuddered theatrically. 'I am certain I am infested with crawlers and fleas, and intend to do something about it before I am seen by my mother. She would have a fit of the vapours, and I can assure you that is not something you want to see.'

'I shall have fresh garments brought to you. The master suite is ready for occupation. Use that.'

She smiled her thanks and walked away as if nothing untoward had occurred. He watched her closely and could see that she was limping slightly. If he ever got hold of the bastards who had harmed her, they would not survive the experience.

★ ★ ★

Mary was already inside and hovering in the impressive entrance hall, waiting for Penny to arrive. 'They are ever so kind here, miss. I'm to take you upstairs so you can be attended to.'

Penny didn't think she'd been into the master suite, but her maid seemed to know the way so she followed her. Her ankle was rather painful where she had turned it at some point during her escapade. She couldn't wait to remove this gown and consign it to the ragbag — after it had been thoroughly laundered, of course.

Her head was itchy as if she already had lice, and she intended to get it carefully washed and combed with vinegar at the earliest possible opportunity. There was that ruffian's blood on her person and her gown, and she needed to remove that as well.

'In here, miss. I've never seen the like.'

Mary ran forward through what would be Edward's bedchamber and out of the other side into the room from which she could hear the sound of water being tipped into a bath. That was exactly what she needed, and she could wash her hair at the same time. The fact that she had nothing clean to put on when she emerged from the water did not bother her one jot. She would remain draped in towels until her fresh garments arrived from the Lodge.

She stopped in delight to see that she was to use Edward's bathing room. The water would cover her completely; she had never been able to be totally immersed apart from the time she had swum in the lake as a child.

'Are there sufficient towels for me to wash my hair, dry myself and then wear until my fresh items arrive?'

Mary giggled and pointed. 'There is no housekeeper here yet, but the foreman's wife is running the kitchen. She has found you one of Mr Trevelyan's nightshirts. It's so large you will be perfectly decent wearing that.'

Her maid seemed unaware that to put on a garment over her naked flesh that had once been over his was highly unsuitable. She looked at the gently steaming lemon-scented water and decided that this once she would disregard her scruples, as she did so wish to use this remarkable bath.

The experience was every bit as

delightful as she'd anticipated. Once she was clean and had luxuriated for half an hour she stepped out, dried herself and put on the nightshirt. Then she kneeled beside the bath and Mary scrubbed her hair and then rubbed vinegar into it.

'I reckon I'll have to do the same when I get the time. I was even closer to them varmints than you were, miss.'

The water was gurgling out of the plug in a satisfactory manner. Where it vanished to, Penny had no idea, but it was certainly going to make life so much easier for everyone. 'Run downstairs and see if there is any more hot water. If there is, you must bath and wash your hair. There's no point in me being free of vermin if you are not also.'

'If you don't mind, then that would be grand. It's men that bring up the water, so you had better not be in here when they come. There's refreshments been sent up for you, and they are in the parlour.'

'I hope that Mr Trevelyan thinks to

send clean clothes for you as well, Mary.'

'Cook has found me something of hers that will do just fine.'

Penny, although decently covered, felt slightly uncomfortable wandering through Edward's private domain wearing one of his nightshirts and nothing else at all. This was certainly a day of surprises.

There were two trays on the table, both covered with clean white cloths, and the aroma drifting towards her made her stomach rumble. She hadn't eaten since breakfast and realised she was hungry. She ate her fill of the delicious food and then stretched out on the comfortable daybed. She hadn't meant to fall asleep, but after the exertions and alarms she had undergone that day, she could not keep her eyes open.

Eventually she awoke to find the sun had begun to set. 'Mary, why didn't you wake me?'

'Your maid is no longer here. I sent her back.'

Penny couldn't keep back her squeal of horror to find Edward had come into the room whilst she was lounging about on his chaise longue with only his nightshirt to cover her embarrassment. Then she looked down and saw there was a soft cotton comforter draped over her so that not an inch was on show that should not be.

'Why are you here?' she asked him. 'Mama will be beside herself.'

'No, sweetheart, she will not. She is cognisant of the circumstances and is resigned to the fact that you will not be returning tonight but staying here.'

She snatched up the comforter and held it under her chin. 'I cannot possibly do that. You should not be in here with me. Where are my clean clothes? Why did you send Mary away when I need her?'

'I shall endeavour to answer. Your maid would have remained, but she was anxious to return the safety of the Lodge and be able to put on her own gown. The one that she was borrowing was far too voluminous and she could not possibly have worked dressed as she was.'

'That does not explain why you are sitting here when you are as well aware as I am that to be doing so, you have compromised us both.'

'I have done no such thing. I am your guardian, in *loco parentis* if you like, and it is perfectly proper for me to be in your sitting room in broad daylight.'

'That is fustian, and you know it, sir. Kindly remove yourself — go downstairs — and allow me to get dressed.'

His lips compressed at her peremptory instructions, but he did as she bid without comment. Once he had gone, she scrambled upright and, still enveloped in the comforter, ran into the bedchamber where she found everything she needed laid out neatly on his bed. When she removed the nightshirt, it was to discover that her twisted ankle had been carefully bound by someone.

Once she was decently clothed, her heart began to slow and she recovered her equilibrium. She prayed that it had been Mary who had covered her up and attended to her injury and not Edward himself. She would die of mortification if he had seen her dressed as she had been.

The only problem now was what to do with her waist-length still-damp hair, which had a distinct smell of vinegar — hardly an attractive perfume. The best she could do was braid it and leave it hanging down her back.

When she emerged from Edward's bedchamber, she heard a longcase clock strike seven times. She could hardly credit that she had been asleep for so long. She never took to her bed during the day unless she had a fever.

If she didn't put her weight on it, her ankle hardly hurt at all. She had only walked a few yards when Edward strolled up and without a by your leave picked her up in his arms.

'You cannot possibly negotiate the staircase with a sprained ankle, my love, so I intend to carry you down. There is a cold collation set out for us on the terrace. I am sure that you are hungry — I know I certainly am, as I have not eaten since God knows when.'

She took a deep breath, intending to protest, then decided she rather liked being carried by him. She rested her cheek against his topcoat and inhaled his unique smell. Lemon verbena soap, she thought it was, mingled with something else she did not recognise.

A gurgle of laughter escaped, and once that was out, she started to giggle and couldn't stop. He put her down gently but kept his arm around her waist. 'Now what? I cannot carry you when you are laughing so much.'

Tears were streaming down her cheeks, and all she could do was shake her head. He crossed his arms and leaned against the wall, waiting for her to recover. It took several minutes, but he had not become impatient.

'I beg your pardon, Edward, but it was the thought that whilst you smell of lemon soap, I smell of vinegar — hardly an attractive perfume.'

His hand came out slowly and she froze. His fingers brushed her cheek and then slid smoothly over her plaited hair. He raised the braid and sniffed it thoughtfully. 'I had wondered why I could smell pickles, and now I understand. I take it this is a family remedy for crawlers?'

'It is what Nanny used when my brother and I became infested.'

'I take it you have quite recovered from your merriment, and it will be safe to transport you the remainder of the way?'

'I have no intention of being transported anywhere. I turned my ankle slightly; I'm quite capable of walking downstairs without your assistance.' To prove a point, she dodged past him, picked up her skirt and all but skipped across the gallery and down the staircase. He made no attempt to stop her, and she wasn't quite sure what she would have done if he had intervened.

She rather regretted having put her

entire weight on her injury by the time she reached the chequered hall. Edward arrived smoothly at her side, and this time when he picked her up she was grateful.

'Thank you, sir. My ankle is not as robust as I had thought. Perhaps there is a bath chair somewhere I can use so you will not be obliged to carry me about the place?'

'I am content to do so, sweetheart. You are far too thin. If you were the correct weight for someone of your height, then it would be a different matter.' This was said with a straight face, but for a horrible moment she thought he was serious. Then his lips twitched.

'You are outrageous, Mr Trevelyan. I am not thin but fashionably slender.'

They had now arrived on the terrace, and he carried her across and put her carefully down on a waiting chair. She forgot their badinage and looked around in wonder.

'I had not realised how spectacular

the vista is from this terrace. With the sun setting over the lake turning the water to liquid gold, it is quite stunning. Thank you for arranging this for me.'

'It was not my idea, Penny. I have not a romantic bone in my body. One view is very like another to me. One of the staff came up with it — more because it is too hot in the dining room than for any other reason, I suspect.' He gestured towards the table set out with a variety of cold cuts, pasties, pies, and other tasty items. 'What would you like me to fetch you?'

'Whatever is there will be fine. However, I would prefer to have the savoury items separate from the sweet.'

He filled two plates and carried them over. He had ensured that they would be alone, as there were things he wished to discuss with her that could not be overheard by anyone, even staff as loyal as those he was now employing.

He poured himself a glass of claret, but she shook her head and had lemonade instead. 'What is it you wish to speak to me about, Edward? Has something catastrophic occurred at Brook Farm?'

He nodded. 'You are too observant, my dear, but I think we shall eat before we talk.'

She was happy to acquiesce and did not indulge in idle chit-chat whilst they ate but concentrated on her plate. She was so like him in so many ways. She was the perfect match for him, and yet she could never be his.

He forced himself to swallow what was in his mouth. His throat had tightened. He was unmanned at the thought that he was in love with this woman and almost certain that she reciprocated his feelings, but they could do nothing about it.

She dropped her cutlery with a clatter and he looked up. 'I am replete. You appear to be having difficulty finishing your meal, so why not abandon it?'

The fact that she didn't ask why he was unable to eat was yet further proof that she understood him perfectly. He came to a decision. The things he had intended to say to her were no longer relevant.

'Sweetheart, I shall not burden you with my problems, but I want to ask you something. Do you love me enough to live beside me as my wife without the benefit of God's blessing?'

'More importantly, do you love me?'

He kicked back his chair and was at her side before she finished speaking. He turned her chair so she was facing him and dropped to one knee in front of her.

'I believe that I fell in love with you the first day that I met you. I have no right to ask this, but I find I cannot bear the thought of you marrying Thorogood.'

'Marrying Thorogood? What maggot has got into your brain to make you think I should do such a ridiculous thing? He would do for Mattie when she is older, but if I cannot be with you then I shall remain a spinster.'

He took her hands and was touched to find them trembling in his. 'Would you do me the inestimable honour of becoming my wife? It will be invalid legally . . . '

'Fiddlesticks to that! If we exchange vows in the sight of God, despite what you said earlier, we will have his blessing. The fact that we cannot be married using your correct title is nothing to me. As far as my family are concerned, I will be Mrs Trevelyan, the wife of the wealthiest gentleman in the vicinity.'

He regained his feet and pulled her up as he did so. She fitted perfectly into his embrace, as if she had been born to be there. He kissed her thoroughly, and she responded with such passion that he could barely restrain himself from snatching her up and carrying her to his bedchamber.

'We had better sit down as far apart as possible, or this will continue to its natural conclusion — something which we would both regret in the morning.'

She resumed her seat. Her cheeks

were becomingly flushed and her eyes radiant. Bentley had intended to ruin his life. In this the earl had failed miserably, as now Edward was the happiest man in the kingdom. His only regret was that his father could not share in his good fortune but must remain isolated and alone in that mausoleum of a house.

12

'I cannot stay here with you unchaperoned, Edward, my love, not now that we are officially betrothed. As my legal guardian it was almost permissible for us to be alone, but now, definitely not. I insist that we return to the Lodge immediately.'

'Before we leave, there are things I must tell you about today. For some unknown reason, we have not got around to that as yet, when it was the prime purpose of my keeping you here.'

She waited, and his expression became grave. Her heart was trying to escape from behind her bodice. What could be so bad that it made him look so? Her hands clenched in her lap and she braced herself.

'There is no easy way to tell you this, darling, so I shall be blunt. One of the men you hit has died. The other is saying it was an unprovoked attack and that they had merely ridden over to speak to you.'

Her dinner threatened to return and she gulped convulsively. She was a murderer. She looked around, expecting the constables to arrive at any moment to arrest her.

He was at her side and lifted her from her seat and carried her inside to the daybed. There he sat cradling her, offering her the support and comfort she so desperately needed. She sobbed into his shoulder, and he stroked her back and murmured soothing words.

'Come, sweetheart, do not distress yourself. The man would have danced at the end of a rope if he had not died already. I was inept in my announcement. I should have said at the outset that the villain's story was not believed and that Mary confirmed that you had been attacked.'

She sniffed, and he pushed his handkerchief into her fingers. She blew her nose noisily and wiped her eyes.

'I'm not to be taken away?'

'Of course you're not, you pea-goose. You are to be congratulated for your bravery and quick thinking. Both Brook Farm and Eastwick have been cleared, and now Farmer Turner has control of the land.'

She rested her head against his damp shirt and sighed. The fact that the man she had killed would have died at the hands of the law did not make her feel any better about it. To have taken another's life was a dreadful thing. Whatever he said to the contrary, she was a murderer, a woman no gentleman should have anything to do with.

Sadly, she untangled herself and stood up. 'You do realise that I can no longer marry you? I am not fit to be any man's wife, and especially not someone as honourable as yourself.'

'You have quite mistaken the matter, my love, but I shall not attempt to dissuade you tonight. You are shocked and upset. Tomorrow, when you are rested and thinking more clearly, you

will realise how this makes no difference.'

'Take me home, please. I have no
wish to discuss it any further. As you
say, by tomorrow things will be clearer
in my head.'

'Bruno is here. If you are prepared to
ride pillion, I can have you back no
time. However, if you prefer to wait for
the carriage . . . '

'No, I shall ride with you.'

'Wait for me in the hall and I will
fetch him. It won't take me long to
saddle him myself. That poor beast you
rescued has become a firm favourite,
and I believe will make an excellent
farm horse once he is recovered.'

'It would please me if you could
rescue all the animals that were in that
place. They did not deserve to be
treated as they were.'

She put her arm round his neck
without him asking, and he whisked her
into the hall. The sun was almost down,
but it would not be dark for a few hours
yet. Time enough for her to put her

plan into action.

On the return journey, she leaned against him, knowing it was for the last time. He lifted her down on their arrival, and she waited for him to dismount and hand his reins to a waiting stable boy.

'Please do not say anything about what has happened between us to my family.'

'I give you my word they shall hear nothing from me.'

'Thank you. I love you. I just wish things could have been different for us.'

She stepped into his arms and tilted her face to receive his kiss. It didn't matter that they might be observed by a lurking groom. Tomorrow she would be gone, and what had happened today would pale by comparison.

Gently she pushed on his chest and he released her. 'Good night, my love. Thank you for tonight.'

'I love you, sweetheart; and whatever you might think now, I intend to marry you.'

He made no attempt to stop her as she hurried into the house. They both knew it had been quite unnecessary for him to carry her; that it had just been an excuse for them to be closer than they should be.

The voices of Penny's sisters and mother drifted from the drawing room. If she went in to speak to them, she would break down, and they might possibly guess her intention. Once she was safely in the privacy of her bedchamber, she rang for her maid.

'Mary, I must thank you for your courage today. I have the most dreadful megrim — I am going to retire and must not be disturbed under any circumstances until I ring for you. These headaches can last for a day or more, so do not be surprised if I do not call you until lunchtime tomorrow.'

'Shall I bring you a receptacle in case you cast up your accounts? I shall move the jug of barley water to your side table so you can reach it if you need to.'

The shutters were closed and the

curtains drawn at the windows and around her bed. There was no point in attempting to leave whilst it was still light. She would sleep if she could, as she would need all her strength tomorrow.

★   ★   ★

When his beloved failed to appear at breakfast, Edward was concerned. He sent word up to her room and was reassured when the message returned that she had a megrim and would be remaining in bed today whilst she recovered.

He wasn't surprised she was unwell. He could not imagine another woman in the country who could have done what she did. To have saved herself and her maid from being violated certainly, and murdered possibly, was the most courageous thing he'd ever heard of.

It might take a little while to convince her that the fact that the man had died from the blow she had given him did not make her guilty of anything apart from being brave and resourceful. He would have killed both of them with his bare hands and not thought twice about it.

He spent the morning with Thorogood going through his plans to improve the land and the lot of his villagers. 'I'm content where I am. I know nothing of society and do not believe I should be comfortable rubbing shoulders with the *ton*. My wards will make brilliant matches without going to London to parade at Almack's like prize mares.' No sooner had he finished his sentence than he realised he had made a catastrophic error.

Thorogood's expression changed. He stared at him, and Edward knew he had revealed his true self.

'That was stupid of me. I am about to trust you with my life, sir. I hope my judgement is not faulty.'

'Nothing you reveal will ever be spoken of by me.'

Edward explained the whole, and his companion nodded as if unsurprised. 'I had my suspicions that you were not the person you are purporting to be, but it had not occurred to me you could be Lord Stonham. From what you have said, you have been accused of something you did not do. I intend to put matters straight.'

'I don't see how you can do so without alerting the authorities that I am still in the country.'

'You must write everything you have told me down as if you are writing a letter. Address it to me; for although we were not acquainted, there is no reason why we should not have known each other despite the fact that you are several years my senior. We moved in the same set, after all.'

'That is an excellent notion. You must state that the letter was delivered to you by hand.' This was a brilliant scheme, and as he spoke he realised that it might actually work. 'Say the letter travelled from Rome and was eventually brought to you by the good offices of a Cornish fisherman. Everybody knows that most of them are also smugglers and are frequently back and forth to France illegally.'

'I am certain it would work. As far as anyone here is concerned, I am in London on business for you. In fact, it might be a good idea for me to take the chest of treasure to a bigger concern than the one you are dealing with in Ipswich. Possibly not your family bank, but another one of equal importance.'

Edward sat back and for the first time since the duel could breathe easily again. He could see that very soon he would be able to take his place in society, and Penny would become Lady Stonham.

He surged to his feet and clapped the young man on his back. 'I have the utmost confidence in you. I should like you to be the first to congratulate me. Miss Bradshaw and I are betrothed. I must go to her at once and give her the good news.'

He took the servants' staircase, much to the shock of a maid coming down with an armful of dirty linen. Even more surprised was Mary, who was busy attending to some mending in the dressing room.

'Excuse me, but I must speak to Miss Bradshaw.'

'She is still sleeping, sir. She gave me strict instructions not to wake her but to wait for her to ring.'

'I shall wake her.' He strode past the maid, ignoring her horrified expression, and called out as he entered the bed-chamber. 'Darling Penny, I have the most wonderful news for you.'

There was no answer. For a moment he was unable to move; then he threw back the bed hangings — and as he had feared, the bed was empty. Penny had run away. There was a letter addressed to him resting on the pillow.

He opened it and cursed himself for being a gullible fool as he read the contents.

Dearest Edward,
I cannot tell you how sorry I am to be leaving you. You must understand

that I would never do so if I had any other choice. I love you and I always will, but you cannot marry a murderer. One day you will be restored to your rightful place, and being attached to me would ruin your life.

Please do not look for me, as it will put your own life in danger, and I could not bear to be the cause of that.

I hope you will explain to my sisters and mother why I have left. Tell them not to worry, as I am quite capable of taking care of myself. They will realise that for me to remain would taint them by association, so they will be relieved that I am gone once they have got over the shock.

I have just over ten guineas in my reticule, which will be more than enough to set me up in a new life.

Forgive me, my love, and find someone who is worthy of you.

The page was blotched, the ink smudged. She had been distraught when she had written this letter. He would not rest until she was restored to him, however long that took. He hurtled down the main stairs and skidded to a halt so he could enter the drawing room at a sensible pace. The first person who needed to know that Penny had run away, and why, was Lady Bradshaw. He was not looking forward to this interview at all.

★ ★ ★

Penny waited until the house was quiet, then slipped out of bed and dressed in a gown that would not identify her as anyone but a respectable young lady looking for employment. Before she had written a note for Edward, she had forged two references purportedly from her previous employers. She used two different quills and two different types of paper and was certain no one would question their authenticity.

The problem was that if anyone bothered to check, they would find she had never worked for either family in any capacity. She had deliberately chosen families that were known to her in the hope that if an enquiry did come, they would guess the reason and not denounce her.

When this was done, she packed a valise with her essentials and was ready to depart. She had sufficient money to live comfortably for a year, to perhaps rent a cottage or become a lodger somewhere. However, she was determined to get a position as a governess so that she could remain invisible.

Perhaps one day, a long time in the future, it would be safe to visit her family, as the scandal should be forgotten. But she could not think of that now.

Initially her intention had been to walk the ten miles to Ipswich before dawn and find herself a respectable lodging before taking her application for employment to the agency in the market town. But after consideration, she thought it would be better to go to

London where she was not known. If she caught the coach from there and not from the local inn, her whereabouts would not be discovered so easily.

When she could not be found after a local search, she thought her mother would resign herself to the fact that her eldest daughter had gone and that it was for the best.

The walk was accomplished in good time, and she was able to catch the nine o'clock coach. She was certain she went unremarked in her plain brown cambric gown, darker brown spencer and ugly bonnet. She made no attempt to interact with the other passengers and kept her face hidden as much as possible.

The coach trundled into its final destination at six o'clock, where she disembarked, glad to be out from the jolting, rattling carriage. She walked briskly in the opposite direction to the one she had taken when she had been here so recently, and soon found herself a satisfactory boarding house.

The landlady gave her a cursory inspection and a thin smile. 'I have two rooms available, miss. Will you be wanting your own parlour, or would you be wanting to eat with my other lodgers?'

'My name is Sarah Smith. I have come to seek employment as a governess in the city. I should like to remain here until I find something that will suit. I think that I should prefer to eat in my room, thank you.'

Penny paid for a week in advance. The sum was a little more than she'd hoped, but it did include full board as well as her accommodation. She was shown to her apartment and was pleasantly surprised.

'This will be perfect, thank you. I shall be very comfortable. Is it permitted for one to walk in the garden at the back?'

'Yes, it's for the use of my ladies. I've got four permanent residents and three, like yourself, here on a temporary basis. You would be most welcome in the dining room, Miss Smith, when you have settled in.' Mrs Rollins nodded and smiled encouragingly. 'I only take respectable ladies. All of them have been in service of some sort or are seeking a fresh position as you are.'

'In which case, might I change my mind? I should much prefer to find something through a recommendation than through an agency.'

'I shall have the girl bring you up something on a tray, as obviously you have missed dinner tonight. Breakfast is served at eight o'clock sharp unless you have made a special arrangement.'

'Then I shall see you tomorrow morning.'

Her rooms were small but well-appointed and spotlessly clean. It took only a few minutes to unpack her meagre belongings and put her night-gown, neatly folded, on the end of her bed. She had eaten nothing all day but still could do no more than pick at the tasty supper that was brought to her. When she had finished, she put the tray outside the door as instructed.

Although she was tired after the long journey, she was desperate for some fresh air and exercise, although the air in London in May could hardly be called fresh. Fortunately, this was a decent part of town, and the noxious smells that they had passed through in the East End were not so pungent here.

She followed the instructions she had been given to find the garden and stepped outside. She had not travelled more than a few yards when she saw she was not alone out there.

'Good evening, Miss Smith. I'm so glad you have decided to join us after all. We always take a promenade in the garden before we retire.' The speaker was a sprightly lady of uncertain years, with grey hair and bright eyes. 'I am Miss Simpson, retired governess, spending my twilight years in the city that I love but never had time to visit when I was working.'

Introductions were made, and Penny was glad she had met all the permanent residents so quickly. One of them, a Miss Brotherton, had only just left her position. 'I gave up my place because the family are moving abroad. I could not face living anywhere but in England. Sir James and Lady Carly are still urgently seeking a governess to take care of their two daughters. I think you would be ideal if you are prepared to travel.'

'I should like nothing more than to live in Italy. I always dreamed of visiting that country, in fact visiting any country. I shall write to them at once and send them my references.'

'I should have remained with them until they left or found someone to replace me, but Emily and Elspeth, the twins I took care of, were so upset about my departure that I could not bear to remain another minute. They are delightful little girls, and I can assure you I would never have left if they had been remaining in Guildford.'

13

Edward was about to enter the drawing room when Mattie called him from the stairs. 'No, do not tell Mama. She will not take it well. Better to try and bring Penny back before we do that.'

He walked across to join her. 'Lady Bradshaw will know Penny is not here when she fails to come downstairs.'

'Beth and I will tell her our sister has a bilious attack and fever and is keeping to her bed for a few days. Mama cannot abide the sickroom and will be happy to stay away as long as she gets regular reports.'

'Your sister is of the opinion you will all be pleased she has gone and taken the scandal with her.'

'We might be as different as chalk is to cheese, but we rely on her and could not manage without her here to guide us. Papa and Ben were absent from home so much that Penny was left to arrange things.' She smiled confidingly. 'Penny is similar in looks and temperament to our papa and brother — we take after our mama.'

'Don't worry, little one. I shall find her. Thorogood is here and we can search together.'

'Mr Thorogood has just left in the carriage; I saw him depart just before I came down.'

Edward bit back an expletive. 'In which case, I had better stir myself and start looking. My promise still holds, my dear. Your sister will be returned to you, although I cannot promise it will be today. She has had several hours' start, and it might take me some time to catch up with her.'

'I doubt that you will catch the coach to London from Nettlested. She will have walked to Ipswich and caught it there in the hope of delaying the search.'

For the first time since he had made Mattie's acquaintance, Edward looked at her more closely. He had thought her as empty-headed as her mother and her younger sister, but she was more like Penny than she realised.

'You think she will go to London and not seek employment locally?'

'You forget, Edward, that although we have gone down in the world financially, our family is well known in Ipswich.'

'Thank you, Mattie. Your information has been invaluable and will save me hours of time. Mr Thorogood is heading for London, too. With any luck, I shall overtake him if I travel on horseback.'

He took the stairs two at a time and told Frobisher that he was leaving. 'I shall come with you, sir, I might be lame, but I am an excellent horseman. I'll have us both packed in no time. I know exactly where the saddlebags are kept.'

He thought it would be sensible to leave by the back stairs. Lady Bradshaw might be indolent, but even she could not fail to notice if he left through the front door with the saddlebag over his shoulder.

There was little point in pushing the horses to their limit, as they could not possibly catch up with Penny before she arrived in town. Therefore, he kept up a steady canter; and as he'd expected, within the hour he spotted his own carriage.

He rode alongside, and when his coachman saw who was there, he drew on the reins and guided the carnage off the main thoroughfare.

'I need to speak to Mr Thorogood. I shall not be long.'

The groom, who had been travelling on the box as an extra precaution against footpads, jumped down and took Bruno's reins.

There was no need for Edward to scramble into the carriage as Thorogood was already out, looking concerned. He took his arm and pulled him to one side.

'Penny has bolted. I should have

realised she might do this. She will be in London looking for employment as a governess or housekeeper. I shall need your help to find her. It will be like looking for a needle in a haystack.'

'If I might make a suggestion, sir, in the circumstances why don't we travel post-chaise? Exorbitantly expensive, but it will get us there in half the time.'

'Good idea.'

The matter arranged between them, Edward remounted and cantered ahead of the carriage to set things in motion. The Queen's Head, a substantial establishment, was no more than three miles ahead. He explained to his valet that the horses, like the carriage and team, would be left at the inn to be collected on their return.

The ostler who hurried out to greet him when he trotted into the yard was only too happy to oblige. 'Your horses will be well looked after here, sir, no worries about that. Will you be requiring refreshment before you set off?'

'No; have the team ready, as my

carriage is not far behind. My coachman and groom will take care of my
horses, and they will need decent
accommodation.'

The man touched his forehead.
'There's rooms for grooms and such
above the stables. Your men will have no
complaint.'

Satisfied he had everything in place,
Edward handed over his reins, collected
his belongings and stepped to one side.
Frobisher did the same.

Half an hour later, they were
travelling at a spanking pace in an
immaculate chaise. It was a tight
squeeze for three large gentlemen
inside, but they would complete the
journey to London so speedily it hardly
mattered. The horses pulling a post-
chaise could canter, as they only had to
travel five miles before they were
changed for a fresh team.

Several times Thorogood glanced at
Edward anxiously. They were both well
aware of the risk he was taking
appearing in London so soon after

Bentley's death. He could scarcely credit it had only been four weeks since that dreadful day — how could he have fallen in love, discovered a fortune, and now be risking everything to find the woman he could not live without?

★   ★   ★

Penny decided to send her letter of application to Guildford by express. It was too late to do so tonight, but she would have it written and ready to go first thing in the morning. This was too good an opportunity to miss. The family would have to leave without appointing a governess, so hopefully they would look on her as a godsend and appoint her without an interview. It would be a reckless expenditure of her funds, but she thought it justified.

She sanded the paper, folded it and sealed it. Her eyes brimmed at the thought that tomorrow she might be leaving everyone she loved to start a new life in Italy with a family of strangers. Leaving her sisters and mother was difficult, but to be parted permanently from the man she loved was unbearable.

Her pillow was sodden before she eventually fell into a restless sleep. She was up at dawn and pacing about the rooms waiting until she could take the letter. She was back in time to be able to eat breakfast with the other lodgers, but had no appetite and no wish to make polite conversation, however pleasant the company.

Perhaps she would go for a walk and purchase some more writing paper and ink so she could communicate with her family once she was settled abroad. As the letter had been sent express, it should be there before lunch. It was quite possible a reply could arrive that very day; and if in the affirmative, it might mean she would depart this evening. She wasn't sure if she was ready to go so soon.

She swallowed the lump in her throat. She must be courageous; do what had to be done in order to protect her family and Edward from being obliged to share her disgrace.

The area she was staying in was pleasant enough, with moderately sized three-storey brick buildings, mostly boarding houses, and all very respectable. It would be foolhardy to wander into the well-known streets such as Bond Street, as she might be recognised. There was plenty to see in her vicinity, albeit smaller emporiums, but nonetheless more interesting than those she might see in Ipswich.

When she returned to her lodgings, the house was quiet. Presumably the other ladies were out seeking new employment or visiting the circulating library or something of that sort. She was now both hungry and thirsty; a young lady could not walk into a coffee house to buy herself some breakfast, as they were the domain of gentlemen.

Her landlady bustled up. 'There you are, Miss Smith. You have paid for dinner and breakfast and eaten neither. Would you care to come into the parlour for some refreshments after your morning constitutional?'

'That would be kind of you. I have no wish to put you to any trouble, as you made it quite clear that — '

'Rules are there to be broken, especially for such a young lady like yourself.'

Penny took a seat away from the window where she could not be seen by any passers-by and was eagerly awaiting whatever she might be given in way of sustenance.

'Here you are, miss. Freshly baked buns, marmalade and coffee. I could bring tea, or chocolate if that is what you would prefer.'

'Coffee is exactly what I like. If you are not too busy, would you like to join me? There is more than enough for two on this tray.'

Her landlady sat down with such speed that Penny was certain she had been hoping for an invitation in order to ask intrusive questions. This was indeed the case, but she was so hungry it didn't put her off the late breakfast.

'I can see from your face, my dear, that you are not leaving this country willingly. An affair of the heart, perhaps?'

'I am a governess, ma'am. It is not my place to become involved with a gentleman.' She hoped that would be enough to prevent further questions.

'I know how it is, Miss Smith. A pretty girl like you would attract the attention of perhaps the son of the house, which would not be popular with your employers.'

'I do not intend to speak of it. Suffice it to say I had no option but to seek alternative employment. I did not leave under a cloud, I have excellent references, and am looking forward to travelling abroad if I am lucky enough to be offered the position in Guildford.' Too late, she realised she had just given away far too much information about her future plans.

'You have applied for the position that Miss Brotherton has just vacated? How fortuitous that you should arrive at the very moment her family are seeking a replacement. Lady Carly is Italian; her father, a count, has become unwell, and Sir James is going out to run the family estates and businesses.'

'Thank you for that information. I had wondered why they were leaving England.' She shook out the crumbs from her gown and stood up. 'Forgive me; I have some letters to write. Thank you so much for the delicious meal. I had not thought to ask — is luncheon provided?'

'Indeed it is. Come down to the dining room at one o'clock sharp. There will be six of you at table today.'

Penny retreated to the privacy of her apartment. It was inevitable that the landlady would know everybody's business, but she wished she had not revealed she had applied for the position with Sir James.

★ ★ ★

The post-chaise made good time, but they arrived too late to begin the search that night. After spending the night at the inn, Edward, Thorogood and Frobisher began the hunt. Edward just had to hope luck was with him and that no one who knew him would be in the area he was searching.

He paid urchins to knock on the doors of boarding houses and remained in the shadows to receive their reports. His valet and estate manager were now looking for Penny as well, and they reconvened at lunchtime in a small coffee shop in a quiet mews near the city.

'Miss Bradshaw would have arrived too late to walk far before finding her accommodation,' Thorogood said.

'We have enquired at all the likely places to the left of the inn she would have arrived at. Now we must do the same on the right.' Edward was sure his search would be successful by the end of the day. The sooner he was away from here, the better. Eventually he would be recognised and his life forfeit.

'I think it might be wise, sir, if I took care of the other matter whilst you and

Frobisher continue to look for Miss Bradshaw.'

'Yes, Thorogood, you do that. Remain in town until you have been successful, and then return by post-chaise. Whatever it costs, get this business settled.'

The young man departed to try and discover the truth behind the death of Bentley, leaving Edward and his valet to continue their enquiries at yet more boarding houses. As before, he lurked in doorways, leaving others to do the actual questioning.

He was beginning to give up hope when Frobisher appeared at his side. 'I think I've located her. At the far end of this street is a very respectable house for single ladies. One Miss Sarah Smith arrived yesterday evening, and she fits the description of Miss Bradshaw.'

'Is she there now? Who did you speak to? Would she have been alerted by the landlady that someone is looking for her?'

'I went to the kitchen and spoke to the cook. Most folk will be happy to tell you what you need to know if you're prepared to pay for the information. Miss Bradshaw is in her room at this moment.'

'Excellent; then I shall go and collect her. Go back to the inn and have the post-chaise come here. It can turn safely at the far end.'

His valet hurried off to do his bidding. Edward was about to make his way to the boarding house when a smart travelling carriage approached from the opposite direction. To his horror, it pulled up outside the very place he was heading for. He could hardly arrive at the same time.

He watched from his vantage point on the other side of the road as a liveried footman dismounted from the rear of the vehicle and knocked loudly on the door. Words were exchanged and then the door was closed. The footman remained where he was.

Edward's heart began to hammer and a trickle of perspiration slithered between his shoulder blades. He had a very bad feeling about this. He crossed the road and began to walk slowly towards the carriage. Then Penny emerged, the steps were let down, and she climbed into the waiting vehicle. The servant jumped back to his position, the coachman snapped his whip, and the carriage rolled forward.

Moving purely on instinct, Edward ran forward and jumped in front of the horses. They were pulled to a rearing halt. The coachman turned the air blue, and the unfortunate flunky on the back was thrown to the pavement.

Edward dodged around the plunging animals and snatched open the door. His beloved was on her knees in the well of the carriage. He didn't allow her to protest, but grabbed her by the shoulders and lifted her out.

'You are not going anywhere, sweetheart. You are coming home with me where you belong.'

'Edward, how are you here? You should not have come to London and put your own life at risk.'

Now that he was certain she was not going to try and escape from him, he released his hold and reached in to recover her valise. 'That is of no account to me. Whatever happens, I shall be satisfied to know you are safe with your family.'

The under-coachman had now climbed down from the box. 'Miss Smith has changed her mind. She is no longer available for employment.'

Penny moved in closer to him, making it obvious she was in agreement with his statement. 'Please convey my apologies to your mistress, but I shall not be taking up the position of governess.'

The man nodded and scrambled back onto the box. The footman who had been catapulted from his position at the rear had brushed himself down and was now on board and ready to depart. The coachman scowled, snapped his whip for a second time, and the carriage rumbled down the road.

This fracas had attracted far too much attention. Several doors were open, and they were being gawped at and discussed in a way that made Edward uncomfortable. Where the hell was the chaise?

'We must walk back toward the inn, my love, and leave London as soon as may be.'

'I wish you had not put yourself in danger, but I am glad you came. I did not really want to go so far away. Are you sure my family will be glad to see me return and envelop them in scandal?'

'They care nothing for such things. They want you with them.'

The sound of wheels on the cobbles made Edward glance over his shoulder. Frobisher had arrived to collect them. He prayed it was in time.

14

It seemed inappropriate to be sitting practically in Edward's lap when his valet was sitting opposite in the small carriage. However, Frobisher was doing a good impression of being fast asleep, which made her feel a little more comfortable. She didn't believe that one should speak as if a servant was both deaf and dumb, so was not prepared to discuss anything personal until she and Edward were alone.

'Exactly where were you going?'

'I had accepted a position as governess to a family who were relocating to Italy.'

The hand holding hers tightened. 'I see. We shall discuss this when we are home.'

'Were my sisters and mama very upset that I had gone?'

'Your sisters knew that I would bring you home, so they have not told your mother. As far as Lady Bradshaw is concerned, you are still unwell with a bilious attack.'

'That makes things easier.' There was nothing else they could say that wasn't confidential, so she smiled at him and then relaxed against his shoulder. Travelling this way was far more comfortable than on the common stage.

Penny slept on and off during the journey, remaining in the carriage when the horses were changed, until they arrived at the Red Lion in Colchester. Here they ate a passable luncheon before resuming their journey.

'We collect our own carriage here, sweetheart, so we have to disembark.'

Penny recognised her surroundings. They were no more than a few miles from home. She could not wait to be back. She didn't regret having made the decision to leave, but was delighted to return. Her only concern was the reckoning that was bound to be coming from the formidable gentleman assisting her from the chaise.

'Frobisher, you are to be our coachman. Are you familiar with handling the reins?'

His valet nodded. 'I'll get you home safe and sound, sir, don't you fret.'

This arrangement suited all of them, as now they were able to converse freely. 'I told you in my letter that you must not come after me, as it was too dangerous,' Penny said. 'If you are apprehended because of me, I shall never forgive myself.'

'It was my decision, sweetheart, as running away was yours. I had thought you an intelligent woman, but to abandon all of us so casually makes me reconsider my opinion.'

'It was not you that murdered someone . . . ' She stopped and couldn't help smiling. 'Although I suppose that strictly speaking, the same could be said of you.'

He reached out and tugged her bonnet sharply so that it slipped over her nose. 'It is not a matter for levity, my dear. Notwithstanding my displeasure at your comment, I must tell you that I was obliged to take Thorogood into my confidence as I foolishly revealed my true identity to him.'

'I am sure your secret will be safe with him. I am surprised that he is not with you on this venture.'

'I was about to explain where he had gone when you rudely interrupted me — that is a habit you will have to curb once we are married.'

She undid the ribbons and removed the wretched hat. 'I was not aware that I had agreed to become your wife. We shall discuss this further, but first you must tell me where Mr Thorogood has gone.'

Edward explained what they thought had happened on the day of the duel, and Penny was astounded. 'If you are right in your assumptions, then that means there must be at least three others involved in this deception, apart from the coachman and any servants who might have witnessed what happened.'

'It beggars belief that Bentley had been about to kick the bucket and had still turned out in order to betray me. He had to have died from natural causes within a day or two, otherwise the trick would not have worked.'

'The whole thing is quite preposterous, and all for revenge for something that happened decades ago. It makes no sense to me. The man who has taken my home and my father's title has done far worse, and yet I would not dream of seeking to extract vengeance on him by attempting to ruin his life.'

'You might not, my love. But I have every intention of giving him his comeuppance. I now have the wherewithal to do whatever I please to whomever I please.'

'Only if you are not discovered. I have been thinking, my love, that if I am to marry you at all — and I have not quite decided on that point — then I will marry you using your correct title. You have already risked discovery by travelling to London to bring me home.

more danger.'

'I should love to do so, but I don't think that we can. I cannot apply for a special licence, as that would immediately reveal the fact that I am not abroad. Neither can we have the banns called in the church, as too many people would hear my name mentioned.'

'Then I cannot marry you at all. It is not because I do not love you; I do with all my heart. But I cannot deceive my family by living with you when I am not legally your wife. Imagine my mama's distress when it is revealed and she understands that I am a fallen woman — little better than your mistress. One day your name will be cleared and we shall be free to wed, but until then we must remain as friends only.'

This wasn't what he wanted to hear, but Edward knew she was right. It would be much easier to be close to her and not be allowed to show his feelings once they had moved to the Hall, which was big enough for them to avoid seeing each other apart from when they dined.

'Reluctantly, my love, I agree to your terms.' The carriage slowed and turned into the drive. 'As you are supposed to be in bed, I think you must go in through the servants' door and also use their stairs.'

'I had already decided to do that. Another thing, Edward — you must no longer use endearments when addressing me. You must use my given name only. Is that clear?'

'Again, I am forced to acquiesce to your demands. Frobisher has driven the carriage around to the back, which is ideal. It is late, and the house will be abed. I sincerely hope we will be able to effect an entry without having to wake everyone.'

Her smile was radiant. 'The side door is never locked. I shall go in ahead of you just in case anyone is awake.'

He waited for a few minutes until she had safely entered the house, and then jumped out himself. Even though it was now after ten o'clock, the two stable boys appeared immediately and were already unharnessing the team. Frobisher was collecting the saddlebags, and he followed into the house, relieved it was silent.

Edward slept soundly and was up at dawn. He wanted to see how things were progressing at the Hall, so rode there whilst everyone else was sleeping. On his return just after luncheon, he strolled around to the front door, which was immediately opened by the footman.

'Good afternoon, sir. Lady Bradshaw is anxious to speak to you. She is in the drawing room.'

He must presume that their deception had been successful, and that Penny's absence had not been discovered, so this was not the reason that her ladyship wished to speak to him so urgently.

To his astonishment, she was pacing

the carpet, not lounging on the daybed. 'Is something wrong, my lady? How can I be of assistance?'

'Mr Trevelyan, I have had the most disturbing news. I dare not tell my daughters for fear of what they might do.'

'Shall we be seated so we can discuss this in comfort?'

She flopped onto the nearest chair, and he sat opposite and waited.

'I received a letter this morning.' She delved into her pocket and held out a stained and creased piece of paper.

'May I be permitted to read it?'

She nodded, and he reached over and took it. It had obviously travelled far.

Lady Bradshaw,

I am writing to tell you that your son, Sir Benedict Bradshaw, did not drown alongside his father but was rescued and brought to this convent. He was gravely ill, had suffered not only from immersion in the water but also from a head injury, and had no notion of his name.

We have been taking care of him for this past year and a half and have been making enquiries on his behalf all this time. Unfortunately, he still has no recollection of who he is, but we were able to discover a sailor who remembers travelling on the same ship as him and his father on another voyage.

Your son is physically recovered but is unwilling to travel back to England as he has formed an attachment to the daughter of a local man and does not want to leave her.

I'm sure that you will be relieved to know that you lost just your husband, and not your only son, in the shipwreck. I hope that you will be able to travel out here yourself and persuade him to return and take up his inheritance.

I have become involved with Sir Benedict over the past month because I too am English. I became a novitiate at this convent when my entire

*family also perished in a shipwreck
many years ago. This is why I was
able to converse with him and can
communicate to you in your own language.*

For a moment, Edward sat digesting
the astonishing information. 'My lady, I
am delighted that your son has been
restored to you. This means that also
your home will be yours once more and
the interlopers will be ejected.'

'Of course I am overjoyed to know
that my Ben is alive. However, I am at a
loss to know how we can persuade him
to return if he does not know who he is
or that he has family and responsibilities waiting for him.'

'I shall go and fetch him back for
you. I shall take your family lawyer,
who will be able to show him the
necessary documents.'

'If you would do so, Mr Trevelyan, I
shall be forever in your debt. To think
that my darling boy is alive. Perhaps he
will come home if he brings this young

lady with him as his wife. I never thought to say this, but however unsuitable she might be, if Ben loves her, then that is good enough for me.'

Penny rushed across the room and threw herself into her mother's arms. 'Our brother is alive? I cannot believe it. It is the most wonderful news — we shall be able to return to Bradshaw Manor and that upstart can be sent packing.' She turned to Edward, her eyes damp. 'I shall come with you. However bad his memory, I am certain he will remember me when I am standing in front of him.'

There was nothing he would like better than to travel to Spain with her, but that would be a bad idea in the circumstances. Then he reconsidered. They could hardly gallivant about the continent as things were.

'Lady Bradshaw, do I have your permission to marry your daughter? Our wedding trip would be to collect your son and bring him home.'

'I knew it. From the moment I set

eyes on you, my dear boy, I thought you would be the perfect match for my daughter. If we have the banns called from this Sunday, you could be married by the end of the month and then set out to bring my boy home.'

His future wife was less pleased than her mama. 'Edward, could we converse in private for a moment? Pray excuse us, Mama. This has come as a shock to me.'

She didn't wait for him to agree but hurried out, and he had no option but to follow her. He left his future mother-in-law and sisters laughing and chatting about having their beloved brother back and being able to return to Bradshaw Manor.

This was another reason he was determined to marry the woman he loved. Once she returned to her ancestral home, she would be lost to him. Even though the marriage, as far as he was concerned, would be in the sight of God and not legally binding, she would remain with him and not leave with her mother and sisters.

He received a fulminating stare on his entrance to the library, but he ignored it and smiled at her ire. 'You should be overjoyed, my love, that your brother is alive. You must see that you could not possibly come to Spain with me unless we are married — that would be even more calamitous for your reputation than marrying me.'

She tapped her foot and did not return his smile. 'We agreed not half an hour ago that we would not be married until we can be married legally. How dare you involve my mother in your machinations? I have no option but to become betrothed to you, but I shall not marry you. I shall travel to Spain with Mr Thorogood and my maid — you will not accompany us.'

He was about to protest, but she raised a hand to stop him. 'No, sir, I will brook no argument or discussion. My mind is made up. As soon as Mr Thorogood returns from London, I shall leave with him.'

'I have no time for these games, Penny. You will not go to Spain without me. Do I make myself quite clear?'

'I have nothing else to say to you on this subject,' she answered. 'Please excuse me; I am going to return to my apartment. I shall not be dining downstairs tonight.'

He stepped aside and she stalked past. As she reached the drawing room, she changed her mind and went in to sit with her family, who were celebrating the good news.

'Mama, sisters, I shall not be marrying Mr Trevelyan. He should never have spoken to you before finding out how I felt on the subject. I have no desire to be married at the moment. If you will forgive me, I am not feeling as well as I should like and am going to go and lie down. My digestion is still unsettled, so I will not be joining you for dinner.'

'You do look very pale, my love. Run along. I do think he would make you the perfect husband, but the decision is yours. If he is not the man for you, then I shall not argue.'

Penny embraced her mother, not something she did often, and hurried away before they could see the tears escaping down her cheeks. There was nothing she would like more than to be Edward's wife. Despite his many faults, she loved him to distraction. But it could never be until he was able to reclaim his birthright. She must pray that Mr Thorogood was successful in his enquiries and would come back with good news.

In the circumstances, she thought the best thing that could happen was for her to somehow find the money to pay for her trip abroad. A few weeks apart would be good for both of them. 'Mary, I am going to Ipswich and you will be coming with me. I shall change into a suitable ensemble. I can manage it myself; you must go to the stables and have the carriage got ready for my departure.'

She quickly changed into a promenade gown and matching spencer and descended to the stables. It would not be dark for several hours, and she thought this was ample time to reach Ipswich and speak to the family lawyers.

She had the precious letter from the nun in her pocket — it was proof enough to set things in motion with regards to the estate. Her intention was to demand an advance on the inheritance she was entitled to. Edward had said he would investigate what had happened to the monies from Papa's business ventures, but it had been forgotten in the general excitement of the past week. If that had been handed over to the family residing in her ancestral home, then the lawyers had been delinquent in their duties.

Once she had the funds for her trip, she would set things in motion, and there was nothing Edward could do to prevent her. There was something she could do for him before she left, however, and she would get the lawyers to take care of that as well.

15

Edward saw the carriage vanish down the drive and cursed volubly. He had no doubt at all that Penny was inside, but where the hell she was going he had no idea. He had no option but to go after her. He saddled Sydney for himself. One of the boys had told him she was going to Ipswich, but for what reason they could not tell him.

He was mounted and about to leave when the unmistakable sound of mounted soldiers approaching gave him pause. For a second he was tempted to flee, as there could only be one reason they were here. He had been recognised, and his days of freedom were over.

The militia had arrived at the entrance to the drive. He urged his horse into a canter and went to meet them. The young officer, the lieutenant, who had so ably arrested the men who had been illegally occupying his farms, raised his hand and his brigade halted smartly behind him.

'This is a sad business, my lord, but I have no option but to take you into custody.'

'I shall not attempt to escape. Where are you taking me?'

'I have been told to take you to Colchester, and from there you will be taken to London and appear in court accused of the murder of Lord Jasper Bentley.'

'Do I have your permission to collect my necessities and inform Lady Bradshaw what is taking place?'

'I shall escort you to the door, but I will not need to go into the house.'

Edward vaulted from the saddle and strode in. Lady Bradshaw and her daughters were sitting together watching the door, waiting to be told what was happening.

He bowed formally. 'My lady, I must be brief. I have been masquerading as Edward Trevelyan, but I am in fact

Lord Edward Stonham, and wanted in connection with the death of Sir Jasper Bentley in a duel. I must accompany the soldiers to London. Miss Bradshaw has gone to Ipswich and I intended to go after her. I hope you will convey my apologies to your daughter when she eventually returns.'

For once, the garrulous woman was speechless. The girls were in tears and equally quiet. He nodded and left them. He took the stairs two at a time, intending to pack some necessities into a saddlebag, but Frobisher was there before him.

'I shall come with you, my lord. I believe they will allow you a personal servant if you are prepared to pay.'

How the devil did he know? There was no time to enquire now, but obviously his deception had been poorly thought out and badly executed.

'Thank you. If you are sure, then I would be pleased to have you accompany me.'

By the time he returned downstairs,

Bruno had been saddled and brought round for his man to mount. The lieutenant did not query this addition to his arrest party — in fact, if anything he looked pleased.

There was nothing Edward could do until he was in London and could send for his father and get the family lawyers involved. He must pin his hopes of escaping the gallows on Thorogood, who held his life in his hands.

At Colchester he was transferred to a carriage, and a fresh set of soldiers rode alongside. Frobisher was allowed to travel with him, but he had little inclination to talk to his valet. The closer he got to his incarceration, the further he got from his persona as Mr Edward Trevelyan.

One didn't speak to one's manservant unless to give him an instruction. He stared right through the arresting officers, every inch a lord. His family was more prestigious and powerful than Bentley's, which meant he was given a certain deference even though he was deemed, in law, a murderer.

He expected to be thrown into a filthy jail cell, but that wasn't the case. The beak he was taken to at Bow Street explained matters to him.

'My lord, it has been decided that you will be able to remain, under guard, in your own establishment. You have given your word you will not attempt to abscond again, and that is good enough for me. You will appear before the court in three days' time.'

The Earl of Rushmere, his father, was a powerful figure and had used his considerable influence to good effect. Perhaps being arrested would turn out to be beneficial and not fatal. He thought he might be bundled into another malodorous carriage, but when he stepped outside saw the family vehicle waiting in the road. The steps were let down by a groom, and he ducked inside.

'My dear boy, I am delighted to see you, but devastated that you have been arrested.'

'Sir, I must thank you for your intervention. How are you here so soon? You do not usually remain in town so late in the year.'

'I received a most interesting letter from a Miss Bradshaw sent by express by her legal people. It arrived this morning. In it she warned me you might have been seen. However, son, it was the other information she gave me that brought me so speedily to London.'

'My man of business, Thorogood, is at this very moment searching for proof. I have three days before I appear in front of the magistrates. We must pray that is sufficient time for him to persuade those involved to speak the truth.'

'I have been assured that even if you are found guilty, you will not hang but be transported.'

'I should prefer that neither option took place. The journey to Botany Bay takes weeks, and then God knows where I might be indentured. It could be a year before I am back in England with my name unsullied.'

'From the tone of the young lady's letter, I must assume that you are entangled with her.'

'I am in love with her, sir, and intend to make her my wife. I intend to apply for a special licence today so that I can marry her before my court hearing.'

'Excellent suggestion, my boy. Then it is possible there will already be an heir conceived before you are sent away.'

'Devil take it! Is that all you can think of? Someone to inherit the title? I intend for her to have the protection of my name and be able to inherit my fortune if anything happens to me.' He leaned closer to his parent. 'I have changed over these past few weeks, my lord, but I see you remain more interested in protecting the title than my well-being. Whatever the outcome in court, I shall never return.'

His father recoiled as if he had been slapped. No one had ever had the temerity to speak to him in that tone of voice. 'If you do not, then I shall disinherit you. The title will be yours, but the estates will go to whoever I choose.'

Edward leaned back in the corner and closed his eyes. The conversation was over. Indeed, from that moment, his life as the heir to the Earl of Rushmere was also done.

★ ★ ★

Penny returned from Ipswich to find the house in chaos. It took some time to discover what had caused such dismay when they should be celebrating the miraculous news that their beloved brother was alive and well and living in Spain.

'He is a lord, Penelope,' said her mama. 'And to think that you refused to marry him, and now it is too late. He has gone. Even if his name is cleared, he will not come back here and mingle with the likes of us.'

'Mama, it makes no difference what

his name is. To me he will always be Edward, the man I love. I wrote to his father and am hopeful an earl might be able to make things easier for him. I was intending to leave for Spain and bring Ben back to us, but instead I shall go to London. Will you come with me?'

To her astonishment, her mother immediately agreed. 'We shall all come. The carriage will be sufficient to convey us to the inn, and from there we shall travel on the common stage. If we intend to take our maids with us, we will require all the seats inside. Therefore, you must send to Nettlested and book our seats immediately.'

She embraced her mother. 'I shall go myself; it will be quicker. I doubt that there will be space today, but hopefully we can travel sometime tomorrow. We shall have to overnight at Witham, as completing the journey without doing so would be detrimental to your delicate constitution.'

Mattie and Beth dried their tears and hugged her. 'We have never been to

London. Shall we be able to attend an opera or go to the theatre whilst we are there?'

'I don't know, but I don't see why not.'

Half an hour later, Penny was cantering towards the village with the groom beside her. It was now quite dark, but fortunately there was a hunter's moon and they could see perfectly well. Whilst the groom held the horses, she marched into the vestibule of the bustling hostelry.

Nettlested was a large village but not quite a town. It was situated no more than half a mile from the toll road and therefore an ideal halt for the coaches to change their horses.

The landlord greeted her by name. 'Miss Bradshaw, what brings you here so late?'

She explained, and he shook his head. 'I can accommodate Lady Bradshaw, yourself and your two sisters, but not your maidservants as well. They will have to travel ahead of you or on the following coach.'

'They can travel with our luggage before us. At what time do we have to be here tomorrow?'

'There is space on the six o'clock for them, but you will have to wait until noon if you want to have the coach to yourselves.' His chins wobbled as he tallied up the small fortune this was going to cost — but not as exorbitant as travelling by post-chaise.

'We shall overnight at Witham. Please ensure that we have the best accommodation available.'

'I shall send word with the overnight mail coach, miss.'

She settled the account and hurried out before he could have asked why they were all in such a hurry to depart for the metropolis.

⋆　⋆　⋆

Penny was up when the three maids left with the trunks to catch the early coach. There was no need for her sisters and mother to be ready until mid-morning. The letter she had asked the lawyers to send to Edward's father would have arrived yesterday, and she prayed he would act upon it immediately.

Whilst she had been in Edward's office, she had also written a reply to the nun, Sister Bernadine, to say that she would come as soon as she could to bring her brother back. She had asked her lawyer to have the letter delivered with a substantial sum of money — half for the convent and the other for her brother for his expenses.

Although she would much prefer it if he returned to England, as long as he was alive and happy, and Mama and her sisters could return to Bradshaw Manor, that would be enough to make her happy. She had other plans for herself. Whatever Edward had to say to the contrary, she was determined to marry him as soon as she got to London, which was why she wished her family to be with her.

A special licence could be obtained

and the ceremony could take place anywhere, as long as there was a clergyman to conduct it. She did not see that as a problem. Whatever Edward had said, she was certain, since there was doubt now on the veracity of the accusation, that the worst that would happen was he would be exiled from the country. As his wife, he would have no option but to take her with him.

Now the war with the French was over, and travelling on the continent was relatively safe, she rather thought she would like to settle in Spain so she could be close to her brother if he decided not to return.

Her mother and sisters were more concerned about the fact that their gowns were outdated, and that their new wardrobe had not been completed in time for their visit, than the fact that Edward might be executed, transported, or at the very least banished never to return to his native land.

'Mama, we shall not be attending parties or mixing in society, so I think it hardly matters that our gowns are not of the first stare. We all look perfectly elegant, and no one could mistake us for anything but members of the *ton*.'

'Where shall we be staying? I hope you have arranged for us to stay in a comfortable hotel. I could not abide somewhere unpleasant.'

'We are to stay at Grillons.'

'Splendid. I have stayed there before and it is a pleasant place. Elizabeth, Matilda, you will be on your best behaviour whilst we are in town. One never knows who one might see at such a prestigious venue.'

The journey was long and tedious, but the closer Penny got to her destination, the happier she became. Her intention was to settle her family at the hotel and then go in search of Edward. She would, of course, take Mary with her. From the one Season she had spent here, she knew that it was perfectly permissible for a young lady to walk about in the good areas of town if accompanied by her maid.

Edward's family house was adjacent to Bond Street, so it would be no problem at all to walk along this fashionable road and then slip into Hanover Square. His father, the Earl of Rushmere, should be in residence by now and should be able to tell her where his son was being kept. Her expedition could not be attempted until the following morning, so she would have to contain her anxiety until then.

* * *

Edward had his own apartment on the first floor of the magnificent house in Hanover Square that had been in the family for generations. Frobisher had set out the hip bath and fresh garments. These contraptions were all very well, but not a patch on the bathing rooms he had installed at Ravenswood Hall. Would he ever see this place again?

Once dressed, he wrote out the information that would be required to obtain a special licence; then he wrote a formal letter and signed it, making Frobisher his proxy in the business.

'I don't care how much it costs. Bribe whoever you have to, but don't come back without it.'

'You'll be wanting a reverend gentleman to conduct the service, my lord. Shall I set about acquiring one of those as well?'

'First I must acquire a bride. I'm hoping that Miss Bradshaw will immediately set out for London when she discovers what has happened. But unless she sends word here, I'll be hard pressed to find her in time.'

'The young lady is resourceful, my lord. She'll be here, I guarantee it.'

His valet took the papers and the purse and headed for Doctors' Commons to obtain the necessary document. He had no intention of consummating the union until after his court case had been settled, whatever his parent might think to the contrary. When he made love to Penny for the first time, he wanted it to be a memorable occasion for both of them and not something hurried and desperate.

It would be time to dine soon, but he'd made it clear to the staff that he wanted a tray in his apartment. There were few books in his sitting room, but he had no wish to venture down to the library to find one as it would mean the possibility of confronting his father. Instead, he would occupy his time by writing a letter to Penny in case, by some twist of fortune, they didn't meet before . . . well, better not to dwell on that.

There were heavy footsteps approaching his rooms, and he put down his pen and stood facing the door. He had no intention of speaking to the earl. There was a sharp knock.

'Enter.' He sounded less than welcoming. That had been his intention.

The door swung open and Richard Dunwoody strode in. 'Good God, man, I thought you somewhere languishing on the continent. Yet here you are. Why the hell did you come back?'

He explained what had happened

over the past few weeks, and his friend was suitably impressed. 'How did you know I was here?'

'Word has spread all over town. The tabbies have been busy. I must warn you that there's been no mention that you are innocent of the charges — as far as the world is concerned, you are as guilty as sin.'

'I have not heard from Thorogood. I'm not sure if that is a good sign or a bad omen. Will you stay and dine with me? I am eating here.'

'I should be delighted. I am not the only one surprised by your reappearance. Your erstwhile betrothed will be staggered to hear you are about to marry someone else when you were professing undying love to her a month or so ago.'

'I thank all the stars in heaven that I didn't marry her — it would have been a disaster for both of us. She needs a more accommodating husband, a fellow who will indulge her, not a curmudgeonly fellow like me.'

'That's as may be, Edward, but if your name is cleared I think you might find yourself obligated to her.'

'She'll get over it. I shall be married to the woman I love and to hell with anyone who objects. My father has been told that my sentence will be transportation not execution. He doesn't seem to believe I will be cleared, even though we have evidence that I didn't harm Bentley in the duel.'

'From what you have divulged, I cannot see how they can convict you. The Bentley family have powerful friends, and I'm sure that it is they who have pushed for the trial.'

'Richard, I want your word that you will take care of my wife if anything untoward happens to me.' He gripped his friend's arm. 'Not only Penny but also her mother and sisters. I must tell you what has just become known.' When he had, his friend was astonished.

'Sir Benedict Bradshaw is aware of his inheritance, but doesn't actually remember who he is or anything about his family?'

'Exactly so. Penny was absent when I was arrested because she had gone to Ipswich to set things in motion for his return — or, more accurately, for her departure to Spain to bring him back.'

'Then let us hope that we can extricate you from this mess and you can make the visit your wedding trip.'

16

Bond Street was quiet when Penny strolled along it with Mary walking sedately behind her. With her best bonnet on, a delightful confection lined in the same dark blue silk that edged her pale blue spencer and gown, she was certain she looked what she was — a member of the *ton*, albeit an unfashionable one.

Most ladies of her class would be snug in their beds at ten o'clock in the morning recovering from the party, ball or musicale they had attended the previous night. They would not emerge from their bedchambers until noon and would then receive or make morning calls for the remainder of the afternoon.

Even if she hadn't known the exact address she was looking for, it was immediately obvious which house belonged to the earl. There were two constables positioned on either side of the front door and another two guarding the archway through which a horse or carriage would emerge.

She increased her pace, her heart skipping about inside her bodice at the thought that she would be reunited with her beloved at any moment. There could not be any possible reason for Bow Street runners to be outside his house if he wasn't inside it.

'Mary, you must go ahead of me and knock on the door. You must ask if Lord Stonham is receiving this morning, as Miss Bradshaw would like to speak to him most urgently.'

The girl curtsied and hurried ahead to do her bidding. The constables didn't stir as Mary ran up the steps and knocked. She remained a few steps from the handsome railings, hoping to be called forward.

The front door swung open. Mary delivered her message and immediately turned and nodded. Penny gathered her skirts and all but ran to the front door.

A liveried footman bowed her in. She had taken no more than a few steps into the vast interior when she was snatched from her feet and swung about in the air like a child greeted by a loving parent.

'My darling lady. I have been lurking here in the vain hope that you might arrive without me having to send out search parties.'

Penny's hands were already clasped around Edward's neck, and she melted into his embrace. His kiss was hard and passionate; it told her everything she needed to know.

Too soon, he slid her down his body until her feet were back on the tiles. 'Come with me, sweetheart, to my apartment where we shall be undisturbed.'

With her hand in his, she hurried up the stairs beside him, not caring that to visit the rooms of a gentleman was quite beyond the pale. His sitting room door was already open, and the room was occupied by a handsome young man with dark hair worn long, in the old-fashioned style.

'Allow me to introduce you to my closest friend, Lord Richard Dunwoody. Richard, this is my future wife, Miss Penelope Bradshaw.'

There was another person in the room and there was no need to introduce him. He was obviously a clerical gentleman. 'You have a special licence? I was going to ask you to get one. Are we to be married at this very moment?'

Edward's eyes blazed, and Penny caught her breath. 'We are,' he said. 'Richard and Frobisher are to be our witnesses.'

This was not how she had imagined her wedding day — no flowers, no beautiful gown, no family present and no church. But as long as she was to become his wife, nothing else was of importance.

There was no time to enquire why the earl was not there, or why she hadn't been asked to invite her mother and sisters. She must presume Edward had heard that his court case had been moved forward to that very day, for there could be no other reason why they must marry in such a hurry.

She stood beside him and they exchanged their vows. The marriage certificate was signed by the witnesses and the curate. She was no longer Miss Bradshaw, but Lady Stonham. She turned to speak to Lord Dunwoody, but he took off as if his coat-tails were alight. There was something very strange going on.

Frobisher made himself scarce and the clergyman bowed and departed, leaving them alone. Penny glanced nervously at the bedchamber door, and Edward laughed.

'Do not look so worried, my love. I have no intention of making love to you until this wretched business has been settled. I wished us to be married so you are protected by my name; so you have everything I own for yourself.'

'Edward, don't speak like that. It

sounds as if you have already resigned yourself to being . . . to being . . . ' She could not continue. Her throat clogged and her eyes brimmed.

He drew her into his arms and held her tight. 'We must be ready for whatever happens. I shall not be hung, but it is possible I will be transported.'

She pushed herself away and stared at him. 'Then I shall come with you.'

'You will do no such thing, my darling. You will return to Ravenswood, or to Bradshaw Manor with your mother. If the worst occurs, I shall go alone. I can only endure the deprivations involved knowing that you are safe and well and waiting for my return.'

Whatever he said to the contrary, she would follow him to Botany Bay. She would not be parted from him for a year or more. Why else had they got married so quickly?

He smudged her tears away with his thumbs. 'You will promise me that you will remain in England until I return.'

She rested her head against his chest

for a second, considering her answer. 'I will give you my word, but only if you do something for me.'

'I will do anything within my power. Just tell me what it is you need.'

'I want to be your true wife. I think I could bear being away from you for so long if there was the possibility of a child. Even if there isn't, then it will make the first few weeks much easier.'

She had expected him to argue, but instead he picked her up and shouldered his way into the bedroom. 'You have given me the two things I wanted most. Did you think I would argue?'

★   ★   ★

Several hours later, Penny woke with a jolt. 'Mama. She will be in a conniption fit because I haven't returned.'

Edward smiled lazily and gently pulled her back so she was once more entangled in his naked limbs. 'Frobisher took care of that.'

She relaxed. 'Two things I have to

know. Why didn't your father attend the ceremony, and why did Lord Dunwoody leave in such a hurry?'

'My father would have insisted that we used the family chapel, and that there was a wedding breakfast despite the circumstances. I believe that Lady Bradshaw would have been equally insistent. Therefore, I thought it best that we married immediately. We shall have a celebratory dinner tonight when they are all here.'

It took a few seconds for this information to register. With a horrified squeak, she pushed him away. 'Are you telling me that my family are here? That they know what we have been doing all afternoon?'

His rich baritone laugh filled the room. 'I think they would both be more shocked if we had not spent the afternoon making love.'

Penny's clothes were scattered around the floor. She had no intention of emerging from the sheets with no clothing on at all, despite the fact that her husband had seen and kissed every inch of her.

He had no such reservations, and threw back the covers and strolled across to the dressing room as nature intended. Just seeing him with the sunlight bronzing his broad shoulders made her hot all over.

He emerged with one of her dressing robes draped over his arm. He looked at her and her breath stopped in her chest. He tossed the garment aside and in two strides was back in bed with her.

They would have resumed their lovemaking if she had not at that very moment heard her mother's voice outside in the corridor. Her desire vanished and she pushed Edward away.

'No, we must get up at once. I should like to bathe before I dress for dinner. I am not meeting your father for the first time as I am.'

He made no attempt to stop her as she rolled out of bed and hastily covered her embarrassment with the robe he had dropped. His smile was wicked, and she was sorely tempted to return to his arms but resisted. 'Am I to assume that my belongings are here somewhere?'

'They are indeed, sweetheart, and your maid is just waiting for your instructions.'

'I cannot bathe and dress with you leering at me from the bed. Is there not another bedchamber for me to use?'

'There is, of course. We have adjoining rooms — go through that door.' He stretched and she couldn't look away. He saw her hesitation and started to move. She turned and ran into her own domain.

★　★　★

Edward let her go. They would have at least one night to share together before he was possibly taken away. He was certain that eventually his name would be cleared, but once he was in the system he became like any other prisoner — just a nameless number. It would probably take at least a year for him to be released and be able to return to England.

He yelled for his valet to have hot

water ready for his ablutions. Although he had laughed at Penny, he had no intention of dining with his father and mother-in-law smelling of the bed.

Thorogood sent word that he was hopeful he would have the proof he needed very soon but would appreciate some assistance in the matter. This was why Richard had left so precipitously.

He walked to the communicating door and listened. His lips curved at the thought of what was going on behind it. The bath at Ravenswood was large enough to accommodate them both, and he had every intention of sharing it with Penny when they eventually moved in together.

There was little point in dwelling on what might or might not be in the future. Tomorrow his fate would be decided. He might be exiled or transported. If the former, then he could take Penny with him; if the latter, she would have to remain at Ravenswood Hall.

Somehow Frobisher was aware he was needed, and mysteriously appeared with hot water and everything else necessary to make him presentable. No doubt his father would be aware that the marriage had taken place without him. Edward wasn't looking forward to the inevitable lecture he would receive when he went to speak to him before dinner.

His wife would take much longer to get ready. He would go down first and then come back and collect her nearer the time. Despite the dire circumstances, he couldn't keep the smile from his face. He was about to go in search of his father, who usually sat in the library with his newspapers, when he heard voices coming from the drawing room.

He stepped in and was astonished to see his irascible parent sitting, rather closer than was seemly, to his mother-in-law. They were deep in conversation. What was equally surprising was that the usually garrulous Lady Bradshaw was actually listening to his father and not interrupting or waving her hands around.

Edward cleared his throat and they moved apart guiltily. The earl jumped to his feet and strode towards him. 'Edward, my boy — congratulations. I cannot tell you how delighted I am that you have married Miss Bradshaw. From everything I have heard from her ladyship, she is the perfect match for you. I had my doubts about the simpering girl you had intended to wed. She would have bored you in a month or two.'

'I thank you, sir, for your kind words. I apologise to both of you that we had such a hurried ceremony, but I feared to delay it a moment longer than necessary. I have arranged for a celebration dinner. Lord Dunwoody and Mr Thorogood will be joining us.'

'Excellent, excellent.' His father turned and beamed at Lady Bradshaw. 'If you will forgive me, my dear, I must speak to my son on other matters not suitable for the delicate ears of a lady.'

'I must go up and change, my lord. I have no wish to be tardy tonight.' She was on her feet and swept regally past, leaving them to converse privately.

'Dunwoody and Thorogood are pursuing a line of enquiry that I sincerely hope will be enough to have the magistrates drop the case.'

'I have called in all the favours I can, and am hopeful there will be a satisfactory outcome. On another matter entirely, my boy, I have offered to sponsor Lady Bradshaw's younger daughters, and they are to have their come-out next Season.'

'Papa, if I am found guilty and transported, then it would be better for them to remain in the country. They will not be welcome in the best drawing rooms.'

'That will not happen. I gather from her ladyship that you are the ladies' guardian.'

'That has no legal standing, as it was done under my false identity.'

'As I thought. I shall take on that role myself. I have always wanted daughters, and it will be delightful to have a house full of young things, parties and musicales.'

If his parent had suggested he was going to parade in his undergarments around the square, Edward could not have been more surprised. This was quite out of character — there had never been any jollity or enjoyment in the house, and as far as he was aware, nothing had ever been considered *delightful*.

'You must change, sir. You will not wish to keep your guests waiting.'

Edward was too stunned to comment on what had just been said — he would need to digest this extraordinary information before saying anything. His intention had been to escort his wife downstairs, but he was still gazing into the fire when a slight sound at the door made him look around.

His breath caught in his throat. He had never seen anything so beautiful in his life. Penny was wearing a pale blue confection with silver sparkles, her hair had been arranged elaborately, and her smile sent shivers to his toes.

'My darling, you look lovely. I was

about to come and fetch you.' In two strides he was by her, and she walked willingly into his embrace. A satisfying few minutes later, he reluctantly raised his head.

'Have you spoken to your mother or your sisters?'

'Briefly. They are ecstatic to be here. Did you know that your father is usurping your position as guardian? Mama seems very taken with him.'

'Whatever happens tomorrow, my love, at least now I know you will all be looked after.'

'I have no intention of accompanying my family to your ancestral home. Our home is Ravenswood Hall, and that is where I intend we reside as . . . ' She stopped in midsentence and shook her head. 'I apologise. It is not for me to say where we are to live.'

'I wish to live nowhere else. I do have an estate somewhere in Hertfordshire, but have no intention of moving us there.'

The evening was everything Penny
could have hoped for. Champagne was
served, and she and Edward were
toasted several times. It was as if
tomorrow didn't exist. Lord Dunwoody
and Mr Thorogood were charming
guests and added gaiety to the evening.

Her sisters behaved impeccably, and
seemed in awe of their surroundings
and especially of the earl, even though
he treated them with surprising benevo-
lence. What did interest her was the fact
that he had positioned her mother close
to him at the head of the table and
devoted most of his attention to
entertaining her.

Was it possible he had formed an
attachment to her mama the moment
he had met her? After all, had not
Edward said he had done the same with
her? Once the notion was in her head,
she could not rid herself of it. Her
mother was an attractive woman; why
should she not find a new love? Papa

would not want her to be miserable.

When the final cover was removed, Penny waited for her mother to rise, but Mama smiled and indicated it was her role tonight. Penny had no wish to spend a moment without her husband at her side; she did not know how long she had him before he might be taken from her.

She stood and was delighted when Edward did so as well, much to the surprise of his father. He glanced around the assembled guests. 'I know it is unusual, but I suggest that we all move into the drawing room as one tonight.'

There was a general murmur of approval. He slipped Penny's hand through his arm and led her across the passageway. She could hardly stare rudely over her shoulder to see how the others were progressing. She was unsurprised when the earl came in escorting her mother. Dunwoody was doing the same for Mattie and Thorogood for Beth.

They remained a short while, and nobody objected when they said their good-nights and retired. Edward had his arm around Penny's waist, and to-gether they raced up the stairs and into his bedchamber. This overlooked the road. The shutters were still closed and the curtains open, letting in the late evening sunlight.

'I shall close these, if you don't mind, before we retire,' she said.

Edward joined her by the window and then seemed to lose his balance. He fell forward with his hands spread on the glass. His face was ashen. What had he seen that had so alarmed him?

Penny peered out and for a second didn't understand. 'The constables have gone. Those men guarding the house are no longer there — does this mean what I think it does?'

His colour had flooded back and she had never seen him look so happy. 'The charges have been dropped. I am a free man. Thank the Lord for that.'

'Then we can go to Spain for our wedding trip and find my brother.'

He snatched her up and kissed her

breathless. 'We can indeed. But first we have something far more enjoyable to do.'

★ ★ ★

A long and wonderful time later, she was resting in his arms when something extraordinary occurred to her. 'Did you notice how taken our parents were with each other?'

'I did. I believe you are thinking the same thing as me. If they were to make a match of it, then our family will be doubly entwined.'

'I can think of nothing I should like more. I can hardly credit that a few short weeks ago I had not met you and now I am your wife.'

His hold tightened. 'I had thought my life ruined, but if I had not fought that duel, I should not be the happiest man in Christendom.'

'And I the happiest woman.'

'And very shortly I intend to make you even happier.'

We do hope that you have enjoyed reading this large print book.

Did you know that all of our titles are available for purchase?

We publish a wide range of high quality large print books including:
Romances, Mysteries, Classics General Fiction Non Fiction and Westerns

Special interest titles available in large print are:
The Little Oxford Dictionary Music Book, Song Book Hymn Book, Service Book

Also available from us courtesy of Oxford University Press:
Young Readers' Dictionary (large print edition) Young Readers' Thesaurus (large print edition)

For further information or a free brochure, please contact us at:
Ulverscroft Large Print Books Ltd., The Green, Bradgate Road, Anstey, Leicester, LE7 7FU, England.
Tel: (00 44) **0116 236 4325**
Fax: (00 44) **0116 234 0205**

WINTER GOLD

Sheila Spencer-Smith

Recovering from a bereavement, Katie Robertson finds an advertisement for a temporary job on the Isles of Scilly that involves looking after a house-bound elderly lady for a few weeks. Hoping to investigate a possible family connection, she eagerly applies. But the woman's grandson, Rory, objects to her presence and believes she's involved with sabotaging the family flower farm. With an unlikely attraction growing between them, can Katie's suspicion of the real culprit be proved correct, and lead to happiness?

AFRICAN ADVENTURE

Irena Nieslony

Amateur sleuth Eve Masters has just married the man of her dreams, David Baker, on the romantic island of Crete. Now they are heading off on their honeymoon to Tanzania. Eve has promised her new husband not to get involved in any more mysteries — but when one of their safari party is murdered, she can't help but get drawn in. It isn't long before she's in the middle of a very dangerous game . . .

COULD IT BE MURDER?

Charlotte McFall

Last year's May Day celebrations ended in tragedy for Gemma with the mysterious death of her Aunt Clara. Having inherited her aunt's run-down cottage in her childhood village of Wythorne, Gemma moves in, hoping to investigate the death, and is drawn to Brad, the local pub owner. But what she finds instead is a dead body, and a basket of poisonous mushrooms that have put her unsuspecting friend in hospital. Can Gemma get to the bottom of things before she and Brad become the next victims?

THE PLOT THICKENS

Chrissie Loveday

The Archway Players are struggling this year to put a Christmas production together in their seaside Cornish town. Adam, a member of the troupe since he was a teenager, is distracted by Gwen, his would-be girlfriend. While Gwen, a health care worker who lives with and cares for her father, doesn't always have the time she needs for the production — or Adam. And when the lead actor is attacked and put in hospital, it looks as if the show might not go on — unless new ideas are found fast.

TAKE A CHANCE ON US

Angela Britnell

In Nashville, Zac Quinn has been a single father to ten-year-old Harper since his wife left years back. Despite his family's urging, he's determined to avoid dating and a social life of his own until Harper is older . . . Rebecca Tregaskas's life in Cornwall is stuck in a rut. So when her American cousin suggests a temporary house-swap to enable both of them to reevaluate their lives, she goes for it. But tragedy haunts Rebecca's past — and when she falls in love with Zac, it rears its head once more . . .